Quoted By The Grey-Haired Diva

YOUR HOLDING MY DREAM IN YOUR HANDS,
THANK YOU FOR YOUR PURCHASE

Cheryl Lynn McPherson

CONTENTS

FOREWORD

My name is Donna Satchell-Spann. I'm a registered nurse. Cheryl McPherson, my friend, my sister, my confidant. When Cheryl asked me to write the forward for her first book I was overwhelmed and emotional. What an honor and a privilege. I met Cheryl many years ago in nursing school, "another book to be written" lol. I remember us pulling all-nighters, whether it be at my home (eating rotisserie chicken) or her home; the beginning, formation of a sisterhood. Fast-forward to graduation day. Cheryl and I missed graduation class pictures (we are not in the pictures on the wall of the school for our graduating year), because we were running late. We were decorating the venue for my graduation party. A friend in need is a friend indeed.

This is a really enjoyable and fun book to read. This book gives you a different prospective on things that we are thinking, but sometimes not sure how to express verbally, with tact, to avoid confrontation and hurt feelings. Every page is crammed full of useful hints and tips so that you can profit from them.

One of my favorite sayings is "**Permission to Speak Freely**". Now there are always individuals in our lives who believe they, and only they, know what's best for us, and they want Permission to Speak Freely. I love that "Permission to Speak Freely" clearly is not an invitation to destroy someone with your words, but to speak it in love. I've asked for "Permission to Speak Freely" recently, using it in love. What I enjoy about this book is that for every saying that you use, there is a biblical backup. You can refer to God's word as it related to those sayings.

Another saying that really hit home for me was "**As a Unit**". It takes a village to get through all of lives obstacles. As I was reading this book (I'm so proud of you Cheryl), "The Unit" brought me to remembrance. It really does take a village to navigate through life's obstacles. I remember when my dear mother transitioned from this life. My mom's service was in Brooklyn, NY. If anyone knows Cheryl, they know she is bad with directions. So Cheryl was like "just give me the address, I'll figure it out". The day of the service my heart was heavy. During the service I just turned my head, for no other reason but to get a reprieve from looking at the casket, and low and behold I saw the Grey Haired Diva. I smiled. After the service concluded she came to me and said "I made it by myself". I stuck to her like glue at the repass, "the unit was there", it takes a village.

I enjoyed the **JLO Method of thinking**. I've utilized it a few times. "Never Give Up on Love". Don't let a past relationship get you down. Thank God for the lessons learned. Leave your ex in a peaceful state and move on to the next relationship without any baggage. The corresponding scripture is 1ˢᵗ Corinthians 13:4-10 (NIV).

This book has a plethora of information and sayings that we can apply to our everyday existence. For every saying you can reference biblical teachings to relate to that saying or experience that we all have experienced in one form or another. This book has something for everyone.
Enjoy the Book

Donna Satchell-Spann, RN

ACKNOWLEDGEMENTS

This book is dedicated to my "HEART", my 1st born and only child, Christian, who I affectionately refer to as "the boy." I wrote this book for you. As a single mother, I want you to know that I will do anything for you and us. You are my inspiration and motivation to do and achieve more. Every chance I get I am praying for you and us. Just in case you ever forget how much I love you, it is now written in stone. I LOVE YOU Christian, and my 1st book is dedicated to you. May God bless you always; may he watch over you all the days of your life. A special prayer that I want you to remember and recite every day God gives you breath is The Prayer of Jabez from 1st Chronicles 4:10:

"Oh, that you would bless me indeed, and enlarge my territory, that your hand would be with me, and that You would keep me from evil, that I may not cause pain!" Remember that God answers all prayers. He is always with you and will keep you from evil if you just simply ask.

I would also like to thank my mom, dad, sisters, brother and besties. Yes, besties with an "s", you all know who you are. Okay, forget it; I will name you: Christine and Charnell. It's a "C" thing. LOL. You are my life savers and I am so grateful to you both. My girlfriend Donna, you already know what it is. To my cousin, Tanika; I love you and thanks for being there for me all those nights when I was crying and driving myself crazy. You were my rock in my time of need and I am so *grateful.* My family has been there for me through it all. The highs, lows and everything in between. I am sure they already know but just in case they don't – *I love you all.*

Lisa, Nancy, Derick, Mom (Joanne) and Dad (Willie). To my Divine Eyes Book Club family: Angel, Brenda, Debbie, Donna, Lillian, Malikah, Monique, Tamara, Taneesha and Tara (RIP).

PREFACE

Reading brings joy and inspiration to my life. I am the president of Divine Eyes Book Club, and welcome you to check out and like our page on Facebook and Instagram. We would be overjoyed if you followed us on both. Through my journey of running a book club and being an active member, I have met some very inspirational people. One author that came through the club said that *everyone* has a book in them. He served as my encouragement to finish the book that I had started 18 months prior to us meeting.

The book I am referring to is the one that you are reading "Quoted by the Grey-Haired Diva." Thank you, Brother Dash, for bringing a message from God to our book club meeting. I have finished the book. Thank you to my girlfriend Charnell Blizzard who came up with the name for this book in less than 25 minutes. I asked her for a name, she texted me back in under 25 minutes and I knew immediately that I was going to use her suggestion.

It is wonderful when you have great friends that love you unconditionally. My friends want to see me win. I want to see them win, and we help each other along the way. I have known Charnell since childhood. We don't always hang out together physically, but we are always in each other's hearts. Love you girl and thanks again for the book title.

This is a fun book with 101 sayings that you can use as alternatives to saying something much harsher to someone that needs verbal corrective feedback. Just like the phrase "Fake News", these sayings are fun phrases that can be integrated into your daily conversation, when appropriate. I hope you enjoy my work. It's my first book, borne of the saying, "permission to speak freely." A longtime friend asked me during dinner if he had permission to speak freely. I said, "Of course."

That dinner served as inspiration to write this book. Permission to speak freely set the tone for our conversation that night. I was not emotionally charged by some of the things that were said to me that night, simply because I had provided permission for the open conversation to take place. This does not mean that, if someone asks you for permission to speak freely, you have to be a garbage can for their verbal trash.

If, at any point, you feel that they are not coming from a place of love, you have the right to put a stop to the conversation and reverse your permission. Life should be enjoyed to the fullest and I hope you enjoy my sayings. Have fun using them in your daily conversations and tell your friends to also pick up the book and enjoy using them.

Integrated in this book are Bible verses that correlate to the sayings somewhat/loosely. I am a work in progress as a Christian. I pray a lot, believe in the power of prayer, and pray that everyone who purchases my book reads it in perfect health.

God Bless and Enjoy
With Love
The Grey-Haired Diva

In 2018 I experienced some difficult times and my dad gave me a Bible. Throughout my childhood, I always went to church and truly believed in God. I always prayed but like most prayed even more during my troubled times. God's words SAVED my life. I decided to include Bible verses in this book, not because they always lined up with my quote's/saying more as a reminder that God is always with you. I used the online King James Version Bible public domain.

1

PERMISSION TO SPEAK FREELY

There will be times in your life when it's necessary to have difficult conversations with friends, family, co-workers and/or your children. Prior to having the conversation, ask for permission to speak freely. Upon their acceptance, feel free to speak. Don't mistake this as an invitation to just loosely run your mouth without any regard for the recipient's feelings.

Their permission is simply a ticket to gently spill your truth and give the person some insight into the situation at hand. They may still get upset about the message being delivered. However, the blow will be lessened when you remind them that they provided permission for you to speak freely.

Permission to speak freely should be used when you want to speak the truth to someone you care about, when you have to break up with a partner, or if you need to speak with a co-worker about something that is difficult to talk about.

I had a friend ask me if they had permission to speak freely. I was intrigued by the very thought of him wanting to tell me the truth. My ears were ready for the truth he was about to impart on me. Instead, I got a barrage of everything he was holding inside waiting for the right moment to unload on me.

It was shocking, hurtful and I was offended by the conversation. When he saw my facial expressions, he reminded me that I gave permission to speak freely. Could I or should I take permission back? I was not in the mood for a verbal browbeating. For some odd reason I allowed the conversation to continue.

It was not easy to hear something that I needed to hear, along with other fillers that were not necessary and hurtful. Unfortunately, the truth hurts, but we need to hear it. The truth will change our lives, set us free and jump-start us into action.

Utilize this saying for good. Don't use it in anger or purposely try to hurt someone. Always choose and use your words carefully. Apologies can be accepted, but the spoken word is etched in the receiver's memory. Speak freely, generously and always with kindness.

This book contains 101 alternate sayings, please give me permission to speak freely and candidly about the definitions I have attached to them. Use them in your daily life, and have fun integrating them into your vocabulary. Use freely and have fun.

I am a Christian, and felt it would be fun to attach some Bible verses after each saying. You don't have to be religious to enjoy this book. Keep an open mind and have fun. I have read the Bible my dad gave me and used the on-line version to incorporate Bible verses. Thanks Dad.

James 1:19-20

[19] Wherefore, my beloved brethren, let every man be swift to hear, slow to speak, slow to wrath: [20] For the wrath of man worketh not the righteousness of God.

Permission to speak freely is not your open invitation to destroy someone with your words. Cruel words can haunt someone *forever*. Speak responsibly.

2

AS A UNIT

For anyone, having a good support system is the best thing in the world. The saying, "it takes a village" is powerful and does not just pertain to raising children. It takes a village to get through all of life's obstacles, and having people who care about you and support all the things that you do is amazing. This is where "as a unit" comes in handy. When you are going through a difficult time in your life, don't go through it alone. Seek the help/comfort of your family and friends, the "*unit*".

When I went through this very difficult time in my life, I turned to my friends and family and asked all of them to pray for me and my son, and to continue praying. I knew that the only way I was going to get through the difficult time was with prayer and with the help of my family and friends. Isolating yourself and waddling in self-pity is never the answer.

Sometimes, you feel like you are overwhelming all of those around you when you have to lean on them in your time of need. That's when it's important to have a team of supportive people in your unit. When one person gets tired, lean on another. Share the love!

A unit also has another side. Violence is never an answer, but sometimes your unit needs to address a situation together. If you and your unit attend an event together, you'll need to leave together or at least make sure that each and every person you came with gets home safely. If someone in your unit has a problem, you'll all have a problem, and it should be addressed as a "*unit*".

Unity brings togetherness, and the world needs more togetherness. Be open to allowing people into your unit. Also be open to cutting people out of your unit. Everyone you meet is not vested in seeing you win. Upon finding out that you have a fraud in your unit, release them. Your instincts never lie to you.

I had someone in my unit who would increase my anxiety every time I spoke to them. They would always point out my faults, and utilized the phrase that they were "just keeping it real." It took me a while, but I finally released them. I told them to go keep it real with someone else. I am no longer willing to deal with their negative energy. I thought I was going to miss them, but it turns out, my life is much better without them.

Don't spend a lot of time with negative energy, let it go and free yourself.

Ecclesiastes 4:9

⁹ Two are better than one; because they have a good reward for their labour.

I am sure God did not want us to unite in the name of violence. However, sometimes you do need a friend to get you through bad times, talk sense to you or to protect you when a horde of people are trying to come for you. God has your back – and so should your unit.

3

MISREPRESENTING THE TRUTH

This is another way to state that someone is lying. The word "liar" sparks up a lot of negative energy. So, rather than get someone all worked up by using the word "lie" or "liar," just say that they are misrepresenting the truth. So many people misrepresent the truth. I am not sure why. I think some of them feel that they are sparing the recipient's feelings.

Unfortunately, **misrepresenting the truth** does not spare the recipient's feelings. It makes them feel disconnected. When dealing with people, the truth is *always* the best way to go. When dealing with others, imagine yourself in each situation, and ask yourself, how you would feel if it were you.

Once you have determined how you would feel, address the person as if you were addressing yourself. I don't want people to **misrepresent the truth** when dealing with me and therefore, I don't misrepresent that truth when I am dealing with them.

I joke a lot and say to people that I live in la-la land. I am the last to know everything. Living in la-la land has a positive and a negative side. The positive side is that you walk around in life trusting everyone. It's so crazy. I am always shocked when I find out that I have been dealing with a **fraud** in my life. That's the downside to living in la-la land. You feel so foolish being the last to know that someone is a fraud.

You're humiliated and feel foolish and wonder if you should change your life accordingly. The best thing I can say about this scenario is, never change who you are to accommodate the world. Especially when you practice being and doing right by yourself and others. Let the good people find you, and remain in la-la land. Overall la-la land is fun.

In my case, I was dating someone who was involved with someone else, and I had no idea. It was heart-wrenching how and when I found out. I kept hitting the rewind button in my mind, wondering why I did not know. In these situations, we wonder, what if? The best I can say is, don't hit the rewind button. You can't change the past. Just hit play; always tell the truth and the energy you put out will come back to you when you get all of the negative energy out of your life.

I assure you that, no matter how many people around you are **misrepresenting the truth**, you will feel and live a fruitful life if you decide to always be truthful. The truth will set you free, try practicing it.

<u>Proverbs 12:19</u>

[19] The lip of truth shall be established for ever:
but a lying tongue is but for a moment.

<u>Colossians 3:9-10</u>

[9] Lie not one to another, seeing that ye have put
off the old man with his deeds; [10] And have put
on the new man, which is renewed in knowledge
after the image of him that created him:

In otherwords, just don't lie, especially to those that you love.

4

ENERGY SNATCHER

This is the opposite of a person who is the life of the party. This person is never happy with anything. They hate the vacation, the waiter was inattentive, their food order came out wrong; they are just never satisfied. When you are happy, they find some reason to drag you down in the gutter. They make everything a major issue, and you cannot satisfy them even if you provide them with a million-dollar winning lottery ticket. Energy snatchers are always negative, and you have to avoid them like the plague.

I have encountered energy snatchers in all avenues of my life. Church, work, home, family, friends and friends of friends. It took me almost a lifetime to learn how to deal with energy snatchers. It's not easy; how do you cut off family, close friends, co-workers and all those in between? It's easier said than done. The best response to an energy snatcher is not to give them fuel for their fire. You ignore, them. When you don't engage, it will lessen the amount of time they stay in energy-snatching mode. You are also indirectly training them to understand that you will not tolerate the energy snatching.

I used to get so annoyed by energy snatchers. I would engage in their energy snatching by listening. I was depleted by the time they walked away, and their negative effects would sometimes linger on for days. Never encourage an energy snatcher. Instead, take action by removing yourself, or simply not responding or engaging in their rants.

In life, you have to always be the star of your own story. You must write your role each and every day, or else the role will be written for you indirectly.

Every morning, I intentionally write the way I want my life to go. I make a list and check it twice. Sometimes, I don't get to accomplish everything on my list, but I definitely try my best to complete it to satisfaction. At the top of my list, I make sure to state that I will not engage with energy snatchers, today or any day – not now, not ever!

Isaiah 40:28-31

[28] Hast thou not known? hast thou not heard, that the everlasting God, the LORD, the Creator of the ends of the earth, fainteth not, neither is weary? there is no searching of his understanding. [29] He giveth power to the faint; and to them that have no might he increaseth strength. [30] Even the youths shall faint and be weary, and the young men shall utterly fall: [31] But they that wait upon the LORD shall renew their strength; they shall mount up with wings as eagles; they shall run, and not be weary; and they shall walk, and not faint.

Don't allow an energy snatcher to drag you down. Stay strong, keep your head up, and remove yourself from their presence.

5

UNSOLICITED LIES

This is where someone offers an explanation for their whereabouts, and you never even asked them a question. The problem with the explanation is; it is a lie. This is where you can tell a shady person upfront. People who start explaining before you even ask, are questionable.

How do you deal with this individual? You can first make them aware of the fact that you know they are lying... oops, **misrepresenting the truth**. This may not help your situation, however, it might be helpful to others that they deal with. The more they are confronted with how annoying their unsolicited lies are, the more likely they are to change their behavior.

Don't be too encouraged though. As Michael Jackson stated in his song that *I love* (Man in the Mirror), you have to look at the man in the mirror if you want to make a change. The only person who can change someone is the person them self.

So, change the way you respond when someone is offering unsolicited lies. Tell them you are aware that they are misrepresenting the truth, and you no longer want to hear their explanation. Move on and accept that this person is just not going to give you what you need from them, which is honesty.

Prepare yourself for the consequences of your actions. People like to marinate in their own lies. You are breaking the cycle of their lies by telling them you are aware of what they are doing. This may be hard to do because normally this tragedy is being performed by someone that you love. You have to gain the strength and be true to yourself.

I had to deal with someone who always offered me **unsolicited lies**. At first, I would beg for the truth. It never surfaced. I went through a time when I thought I was going crazy and perhaps overreacting. Finally, I realized that my gut was not misleading me. A lie is a lie, no matter how it presents itself. A lie is also still a lie, even when it's mixed with some truths.

Decide how you want to live your life and what type of people you want in your life. This will help you to rid yourself of the people you don't want in your life more quickly. Rid yourself of those who constantly present unsolicited lies. It's not worth it.

<u>Exodus 20:16</u>

[16] And unto Sarah he said, Behold, I have given thy brother a thousand pieces of silver: behold, he is to thee a covering of the eyes, unto all that are with thee, and with all other: thus she was reproved.

The Bible has spoken! Do I need to say more? Lying is never good.

6

EDUCATED STUPIDITY

Educated stupidity is when you meet someone with a ton of degrees, but yet they don't utilize their brain or education to make sense of anything that they do. They speak before they think. They use big words in an attempt to deflect you from the issue at hand. They make you want to call the university that issued the degree and begin the process of canceling the degree.

Avoid these people like the plague. Let them know that if they don't quit, you will call the school of higher learning and start a petition to annul their degree. It makes no sense for a person to spend all that money on education and not put it to good use. I am a firm believer that people should self-educate and additionally receive a degree of higher learning. This is the start to a person becoming well rounded.

I once dealt with someone who had earned their master's degree; a smart individual, but they misrepresented the truth all the time and practiced educated stupidity. I was baffled by the entire process. One thing I learned from an old trainer of mine is, when it comes to people you are involved with intimately, remember when going through the jungle with them, _you chose them_. So, you have to ask yourself, "what was going on in my head at the time when I met this person? Why have I put up with all the nonsense?" You are always a willing participant in the nonsense you allow to take place in your life.

I assure you; in life, your _self-esteem_ is everything, and it will _directly or indirectly_ impact all of the decisions you make. Also understand that indecision is also a decision. You have to be the author and creator of your own life. Rid yourself of people who practice educated stupidity. You have no time for the nonsense, and you don't want your thinking to be affected by their stupidity.

Ecclesiastes 7:25

[25] I applied mine heart to know, and to search,
and to seek out wisdom, and the reason of things,
and to know the wickedness of folly, even of
foolishness and madness:

7

GREEN ZONE

The green zone is your calm place. In life you should never allow anyone or anything to take you out of your calm zone. This is the place you should be in 95-100% of the time. I know it is easier said than done. We all have trigger points. I have mine, and most of the time our loved ones are the people who can take us out of our calm zone.

Some tips for staying in the calm zone; take a minute before you respond when someone ticks you off. Walk away from the situation. Pray to have a closed mouth when dealing with people who try to drag you down. You can learn to rise above craziness and remain in the calm zone.

YELLOW ZONE

You are losing your calmness. This is where you are on the fence and have the option to bring yourself back to the calm zone or venture on the wild side and end up in the red zone. I urge you to try your best to get back to the green zone. The green zone is where you belong. It's your happy place. Let no one or nothing take you from your happy place. The yellow zone is where you yield. It's a warning for you to stop and disengage. I've been in the yellow zone plenty of times. There have been times when I've told myself ahead of time, "I will not go there." However, the person will say something crazy and *yikes, I respond*. Practice makes perfect. The more you practice shutting your mouth, the more you will get better at ignoring the triggers.

RED ZONE

You're on FIRE! *Oh my!* You have lost control. All of your efforts to remain calm in the green zone were lost in translation. Forgive yourself and disengage as soon as you can. It's imperative to your sanity. Apologize to yourself for losing it and apologize to the person, no matter who was right or wrong. Your life, health and wellbeing depend on you remaining calm and practicing self-control in your life.

<u>Philippians 4:6-7</u>

[6] Be careful for nothing; but in every thing by prayer and supplication with thanksgiving let your requests be made known unto God. [7] And the peace of God, which passeth all understanding, shall keep your hearts and minds through Christ Jesus.

Ask God to help you remain calm and he will help you.

8

DON'T MAKE ME ANGRY, BECAUSE YOU WON'T LIKE ME WHEN I AM ANGRY

A quote from The Incredible Hulk. Growing up, I loved this TV series. Bruce Banner would always warn people ahead of time, "don't make me angry, because you will not like me when I am angry." We all turn into our alter ego when our buttons are pushed. This statement is useful when you want to warn someone to calm down, back down and give you a minute to regroup. Let them know that you don't want to go off on them but they are taking you there. It's a playful statement that can serve as a warning to someone to cut it out before the situation goes to the left, and neither one of you can recover.

I love to stay in my Zen moment – the green zone. That is when I am the most peaceful and when I have the most fun in my life. Unfortunately, though, there are people who just want to push your buttons. I read somewhere that life is more about how you react to the things that are presented to you, versus what is presented. Social media allows us to be part of a perfect stranger's life. Through a friend of a friend you can find out the most intimate things about a perfect stranger. A man I did not know personally suffered a medical condition that resulted in him having to have his leg amputated. He posted something that was very inspirational. He wasn't negative or sad. He said God saved him and he was still going to continue to do the things he loved in life.

I thought, *here is a man who is facing a real-life challenge, and he is still remaining upbeat and positive!* A perfect stranger's story saved my life. It confirmed to me that I have to always be in control of the way I respond to people who treat me badly, and those who talk to me unkindly, or who try to take me down some path I do not want to go. First, I will give them a polite warning, "please don't make me angry." If they continue on with their pursuit of unhappiness, I will try my best to remove myself from the situation.

There will be times when you will have to show them who they are dealing with, and bring out the Bruce Banner in you. Tell people off only as a last resort. Always maintain you're cool. May Bruce Banner only show up when the person has pushed your last and final button.

John 14:27

27 Peace I leave with you, my peace I give unto you: not as the world giveth, give I unto you. Let not your heart be troubled, neither let it be afraid.

9

THE FACTS AS I SEE THEM

At one of our family gatherings a group of family members were sitting together chatting about anything and everything. My sister Nancy and I were telling the story about one of our NYC adventures; she told the story one way, and I told it another.

As I was trying to convince my family to believe my side of the story, my brother stepped in. He called me by my nickname, Checkie. He said, "Those are the facts, as Nancy sees them." I had an "aha moment." The facts as I see them; does not mean that what the person is saying is not true. It is just their recollection of the truth. Let them have it and move on. Move on, as long as it is not a legal situation; don't try to force a stubborn person to see things your way. Agree to disagree, because you will keep your sanity that way.

However, if you are dealing with a legal situation, then by all means discuss everything to make sure the truth prevails. When it is not a legal situation, understand that the other party is telling *their truth*. They are providing you with information seen through their jaded eyes. Let them tell their story. It is not worth your time and energy to combat their truth, unless you are just having a little fun. In that case, give the person a challenge and debate the story to your heart's content.

Matthew 18:15-17

[15] Moreover if thy brother shall trespass against thee, go and tell him his fault between thee and him alone: if he shall hear thee, thou hast gained thy brother. [16] But if he will not hear thee, then take with thee one or two more, that in the mouth of two or three witnesses every word may be established. [17] And if he shall neglect to hear them, tell it unto the church: but if he neglect to hear the church, let him be unto thee as an heathen man and a publican.

Romans 14:1

[1] Him that is weak in the faith receive ye, but not to doubtful disputations.

10

DUMP AND RELEASE

Whether you are religious or not, you have to find somewhere, other than a friend or significant-other, where you can dump and release your problems, fears and thorns in your side, and _never_ pick them up again. I believe in God, and there are times when I bring all of my troubles to him for resolution. Then, if I feel he is not resolving the situation quick enough, I go back and try to resolve it myself.

I started writing this book in 2017. I decided to complete it this year, 2020. I promised myself that everything I give to God, I will never pick up again, ever. Looking back at the past is never good. Use the rear-view mirror for driving only. I love the author, Wayne Dyer. You have to read some of his books. However, he always advises to live in the now. Live in the now because it is the only thing that really matters. Let go of the past, enjoy the moment and embrace the future.

Exodus 14:14

[14] The LORD shall fight for you, and ye shall hold your peace.

Dump and release it. God has your back. He will resolve all of your battles better than you can. I have watched God work out all the things I asked, and then some. I would avoid praying sometimes because I convinced myself that I did not know how to access God. Just a heads up; there is no right or wrong way to pray. Talk to God like you are having a conversation with your friend. He hears you. He will listen to you and if you have the faith of a mustard seed, he will respond to you. I would say I promise, however, He promises that you won't regret it.

Luke 17:5-6

[5] And the apostles said unto the Lord, Increase our faith. [6] And the Lord said, If ye had faith as a grain of mustard seed, ye might say unto this sycamine tree, Be thou plucked up by the root, and be thou planted in the sea; and it should obey you.

Matthew 17:20

[20] And Jesus said unto them, Because of your unbelief: for verily I say unto you, If ye have faith as a grain of mustard seed, ye shall say unto this mountain, Remove hence to yonder place; and it shall remove; and nothing shall be impossible unto you.

Mark 4:30-32

[30] And he said, Whereunto shall we liken the kingdom of God? or with what comparison shall we compare it? [31] It is like a grain of mustard seed,

which, when it is sown in the earth, is less than all the seeds that be in the earth: [32] But when it is sown, it groweth up, and becometh greater than all herbs, and shooteth out great branches; so that the fowls of the air may lodge under the shadow of it.

Trust in the God who created us. I finally did and my life became magical.

11

LIMITED FREEDOM

Perhaps you have a friend that is locked up, behind bars, incarcerated. No need for details about what they did to find themselves in such an unfortunate situation. When someone asks you where they are and you don't want to answer or explain, just say they are unavailable right now because of their limited freedom. No further explanation required.

Limited freedom can also be self-imposed. Sometimes, people's limited freedom is self-imposed. We trap ourselves in our own body, minds and souls. Our inner voice has us thinking we can't, won't and never will. Free your mind and the rest will follow. Try meditation to help quiet the outer/inner voices and negative thoughts. This will help you hear the true voice of God. I had to revamp and do this for myself. You've got this. Believe in yourself.

Galatians 5:13

13 For, brethren, ye have been called unto liberty;
only use not liberty for an occasion to the flesh,
but by love serve one another.

Galatians 5:1

[15] Stand fast therefore in the liberty wherewith Christ hath made us free, and be not entangled again with the yoke of bondage.

John 8:36

[36] If the Son therefore shall make you free, ye shall be free indeed.

Romans 8:2

[2] For the law of the Spirit of life in Christ Jesus hath made me free from the law of sin and death.

12

EMOTIONALLY HIJACKED

This is when people disrupt your day with their emotional nonsense. They send you a text, make a phone call and intrude on your happy day, moment, time and head space; sometimes, even though you have every intention not to allow this intrusion to take over your day. You find yourself engaging in the nonsense. We are all human. When you find yourself falling into the trap of being emotionally hijacked, bring yourself back to the moment and disengage from the verbal, written and nonverbal back-and-forth with them.

It's not worth it. Do your best to disassociate yourself from people who emotionally hijack you on a regular basis. I had a girlfriend with whom I was friends for over 15 years. Every time she called to check on me, it was nothing but negativity. After our conversations, I was drained, emotionally robbed and feeling bad about myself. It was hard, but I had to divorce myself from her. Friends should leave you feeling full and not empty. Never feel guilty about dumping someone who just drains you, versus filling you up. I did not miss her as much as I thought I would. We are better off without each other.

Proverbs 16:32

32 He that is slow to anger is better than the mighty; and he that ruleth his spirit than he that taketh a city.

Philippians 4:7

7 And the peace of God, which passeth all understanding, shall keep your hearts and minds through Christ Jesus.

13

TRUE STORY

There are times when friends, family members and total strangers provide useful advice. The advice is sometimes a new concept. Other times it is something you are aware of and know it is the right thing to do, but have just not taken action. You can acknowledge that it is a **true story**. They are telling you facts that you need to hear and take action on. **True story** means, I've got you, I hear you, and I am going to take action using the information you shared with me.

People come into your life for a reason, season or a lifetime. Don't hold on to someone who came into your life for a reason, and be strong enough to let go of them when the season arises, so that you can get to the person you are supposed to spend your lifetime with.

John 14:6

⁶ Jesus saith unto him, I am the way, the truth, and the life: no man cometh unto the Father, but by me.

John 4:24

²⁴ God is a Spirit: and they that worship him must worship him in spirit and in truth.

1 John 3:18

¹⁸ My little children, let us not love in word, neither in tongue; but in deed and in truth.

John 8:31-32

³¹ Then said Jesus to those Jews which believed on him, If ye continue in my word, then are ye my disciples indeed; ³² And ye shall know the truth, and the truth shall make you free.

14

EMOTIONAL BAGGAGE

Life is to be lived. As we go through life, things happen to us. I heard that Tony Robbins, a phenomenal motivational speaker, said, "What if you look at life like things do not happen *to you*, but they happened *for you*.

Sometimes, we miss out on all the things God is trying to bless us with because we have all this emotional baggage that we are carrying around and we unload it on the new blessing in our life. That blessing ends up taking the next flight out of our lives because we are just too much to deal with. Don't let emotional baggage from the past destroy your future. If you have to attend counseling, meditate, write in a journal, send the person who wronged you a letter, or ask for forgiveness from someone you might have wronged – just do it. But whatever you do, don't let the emotional baggage destroy your future.

John 10:10

[10] The thief cometh not, but for to steal, and to kill, and to destroy: I am come that they might have life, and that they might have it more abundantly.

Don't let the emotional baggage be a thief in the night and steal your future. Recognize it and address it ASAP. Your older self will thank you later.

Romans 12:17-21

[17] So then faith cometh by hearing, and hearing by the word of God. [18] But I say, Have they not heard? Yes verily, their sound went into all the earth, and their words unto the ends of the world. [19] But I say, Did not Israel know? First Moses saith, I will provoke you to jealousy by them that are no people, and by a foolish nation I will anger you. [20] But Esaias is very bold, and saith, I was found of them that sought me not; I was made manifest unto them that asked not after me. [21] But to Israel he saith, All day long I have stretched forth my hands unto a disobedient and gainsaying people.

Matthew 18:21-22

[21] Then came Peter to him, and said, Lord, how oft shall my brother sin against me, and I forgive him? till seven times? [22] Jesus saith unto him, I say not unto thee, Until seven times: but, Until seventy times seven.

In otherwords always forgive. Forgive over and over again. Forgiveness is a selfish gift.

15

THE FRANK SINATRA SYNDROME

This is for all those people who insist on doing it their way. I get it – everyone should follow their dreams, and go after their goals. That is a wonderful thing. However, there are many situations where the rules have to be followed; for instance, at work. In your own personal life, if you are interested, go for it; do what Frank sang in his song, My Way, and do it your way.

However, in a relationship or work situation, you have to conform with certain "rules of the road." Conform, or find yourself on the outside, most of the time. Disclaimer: when I say the Frank Sinatra syndrome, I am not referring to the man himself. I am just referring to the song. Here are some of the lyrics of the song, My Way;

And now, the end is near
and so I face the final curtain
my friend, I'll say it clear
I'll state my case, of which I'm certain
I've lived a life that's full
I traveled each and every highway
And more, much more than this, I did it my way.

Now I will say this; there are times when you *must* and I mean _must_ embrace the Frank Sinatra syndrome. When you have a dream you want to follow, let no man stop you, including yourself. Remember these words by Frank Sinatra;

Regrets, I've had a few
But then again, too few to mention
I did what I had to do and saw it
through without exemption
I planned each charted course,
each careful step along the byway
And more, much more than this, I did it my way.

Have no regrets. Understand that God makes no mistakes. Learn from your past and make tomorrow a *greater brighter day. Do it your way.*

<u>Colossians 3:23-24</u>

[23] And whatsoever ye do, do it heartily, as to the Lord, and not unto men; [24] Knowing that of the Lord ye shall receive the reward of the inheritance: for ye serve the Lord Christ.

16

THE JLO METHOD

This means never give up on love. I love the way Jennifer Lopez appears to gracefully move on when a relationship is over. She and her ex-lovers never seem to degrade each other via social media, etc. They end their relationship in peace and she moves on to give love another try with someone else. I think this is how we should all view love. Don't let a past failed relationship get you down. Thank God for the lessons learned. Leave your ex in a peaceful state and move on to the next relationship without any emotional baggage.

Unfortunately, a lot of us have been through some painful relationships; mother/daughter, father/son, husband/wife, girlfriend/boyfriend and/or friend/friend. The pain from a broken heart can debilitate you. Don't let it. God makes no mistakes, maybe the pain intended to help you can grow and become a better person. Work through the pain, learn how to do better in the next relationship, and be open, ready and willing to give and receive love.

1 Corinthians 16:14

[14] Let all your things be done with charity.

1 John 4:19

¹⁹ We love him, because he first loved us.

1 Corinthians 13:4-10

⁴ Charity suffereth long, and is kind; charity envieth not; charity vaunteth not itself, is not puffed up, ⁵ Doth not behave itself unseemly, seeketh not her own, is not easily provoked, thinketh no evil; ⁶ Rejoiceth not in iniquity, but rejoiceth in the truth; ⁷ Beareth all things, believeth all things, hopeth all things, endureth all things. ⁸ Charity never faileth: but whether there be prophecies, they shall fail; whether there be tongues, they shall cease; whether there be knowledge, it shall vanish away. ⁹ For we know in part, and we prophesy in part. ¹⁰ But when that which is perfect is come, then that which is in part shall be done away.

17

BARBIE AND KEN

Sometimes, in between relationships, a female or male may need a Ken and someone out there may need a Barbie. This is strictly platonic, not a-friends-with benefits relationship. This is two friends who have agreed to be each other's date at different events; to see a movie together, or have lunch or dinner together, and nothing more. You never want to sleep with Ken or vice versa. This person should be your bestie. They can be the same sex or the opposite sex, whichever you prefer. Understand that crossing the line and sleeping with them will change the dynamic of your relationship. Be sure you want to take the risk prior to jumping into the pond. We all need someone that we can call on when we are in between relationships. Secure yours ahead of time. That way, you will never have to go searching if you are in between relationships.

Hebrews 13:4

[4] Marriage is honourable in all, and the bed undefiled: but whoremongers and adulterers God will judge..

Listen, I believe in marriage and pray that one day I will be lucky enough to get married. In the meantime, I need Ken to accompany me at different events and be my friend while I do not have a significant other.

John 15:12-15

[12] This is my commandment, That ye love one another, as I have loved you. [13] Greater love hath no man than this, that a man lay down his life for his friends. [14] Ye are my friends, if ye do whatsoever I command you. [15] Henceforth I call you not servants; for the servant knoweth not what his lord doeth: but I have called you friends; for all things that I have heard of my Father I have made known unto you.

Side note: a Ken can never be an ex that you had sex with in the past. Why? Because youmay be tempted to cross the lines every now and then and that will not be good.

18

UNAUTHORIZED THREESOME

This is when your significant other cheats, and you have no idea. They have dragged you into this unauthorized threesome, because when your partner has slept with someone else this directly and indirectly affects you. That is why you need to protect yourself. If you think your partner is stepping out on you, they probably are. Cut your losses and move on. You will be better off without a cheater in your life.

An unauthorized threesome can be extremely harmful to your health.

1 Corinthians 7:3-5

3 Let the husband render unto the wife due benevolence: and likewise also the wife unto the husband. 4 The wife hath not power of her own body, but the husband: and likewise also the husband hath not power of his own body, but the wife. 5 Defraud ye not one the other, except it be with consent for a time, that ye may give yourselves to fasting and prayer; and come together again, that Satan tempt you not for your incontinency.

<u>**Proverbs 5:17-23**</u>

[17] Let them be only thine own, and not strangers' with thee. [18] Let thy fountain be blessed: and rejoice with the wife of thy youth. [19] Let her be as the loving hind and pleasant roe; let her breasts satisfy thee at all times; and be thou ravished always with her love. [20] And why wilt thou, my son, be ravished with a strange woman, and embrace the bosom of a stranger? [21] For the ways of man are before the eyes of the LORD, and he pondereth all his goings. [22] His own iniquities shall take the wicked himself, and he shall be holden with the cords of his sins. [23] He shall die without instruction; and in the greatness of his folly he shall go astray.

In others words a woman should only sleep with her husband. Trust me I am not judging. I am a "single" mother. Never married. We all fall short of the grace of God. However, we should try every day of our lives to do better and be better.

19

MESSY

This is a person that insists on starting stuff. They are in the midst of everything. When you get to the root of a problem, their name always comes up. A messy person is someone that you need to release from your life. They are toxic, and you have no business allowing them to remain in your life. They are energy drainers. _As soon as you realize that you are dealing with a messy person, dump them like a bad habit._

Messy

- You tell them something in confidence, and they tell everyone.
- They play both sides of the fence.
- They make sure no one in a group setting likes you, by feeding them negative information about you in secret.
- They secretly want to see your demise, rather than seeing you win.
- The try to over-talk you in every conservation.
- They have a need to be right all the time.

- They are in competition with you and you have no idea or reason why.

Hebrews 13:5

[5] Let your conversation be without covetousness; and be content with such things as ye have: for he hath said, I will never leave thee, nor forsake thee.

2 Corinthians 12:9

[9] And he said unto me, My grace is sufficient for thee: for my strength is made perfect in weakness. Most gladly therefore will I rather glory in my infirmities, that the power of Christ may rest upon me.

Romans 10:9

[9] That if thou shalt confess with thy mouth the Lord Jesus, and shalt believe in thine heart that God hath raised him from the dead, thou shalt be saved.

Isaiah 41:10

[10] Fear thou not; for I am with thee: be not dismayed; for I am thy God: I will strengthen thee; yea, I will help thee; yea, I will uphold thee with the right hand of my righteousness.

20

NECESSARY TEARS

There are periods in your life when you just have to cry, day and night. It is okay. Tears are cleansing to the soul. Cleanse your soul with your tears. However, don't cry over a person or situation too long. God removed them from your life for a reason. Go through your pain and heal yourself as quickly as possible. Take up yoga, do meditation. Get yourself together. Time waits for no one, so give yourself a necessary tear cleansing period of 24-48 hours. No more than one week. After that, do whatever is necessary to pull yourself together. You are worth it.

Revelation 21:4

[4] And God shall wipe away all tears from their eyes; and there shall be no more death, neither sorrow, nor crying, neither shall there be any more pain: for the former things are passed away.

Isaiah 41:10

[10] Fear thou not; for I am with thee: be not dismayed; for I am thy God: I will strengthen

thee; yea, I will help thee; yea, I will uphold thee
with the right hand of my righteousness.

<u>John 11:35</u>

[35] Jesus wept.

21

FRIENDS WITH BENEFITS (FWB)

We talked about Barbie and Ken earlier. They are platonic friends. Now, we already know that FWBs are not platonic friends. You can have an FWB, but you need to be able to handle the fact that you are just an FWB. Don't be fooled by the movie Friends with Benefits starring Justin Timberlake and the beautiful Mila Kunis. They end up being a couple by the end of the movie, which doesn't always happen in real life. FWBs usually remain FWBs for life. Sometimes, someone develops feelings, and the other person has to remind them that they knew what they were getting into when the relationship started.

This can be a painful situation, if you are not able to control your feelings. I don't encourage these types of relationships for many reasons. Sex should not be taken lightly. Most people are not able to enter a sexual relationship without developing some type of feelings. I encourage you to proceed with this type of relationship with *extreme caution*.

Loneliness is a real feeling, and it can make you accept and do some crazy things. Try your best to fight through the loneliness. Having an FWB can temporarily decrease your feeling of being alone, but it will never satisfy your need for love. Hold out as best you can for that true love that you deserve. However, if you are strong enough, go for it and have a little fun with your FWB.

John 15:13

13 Greater love hath no man than this, that a man lay down his life for his friends.

Ecclesiastes 4:9-12

9 Two are better than one; because they have a good reward for their labour. 10 For if they fall, the one will lift up his fellow: but woe to him that is alone when he falleth; for he hath not another to help him up. 11 Again, if two lie together, then they have heat: but how can one be warm alone? 12 And if one prevail against him, two shall withstand him; and a threefold cord is not quickly broken.

22

LOVELESS RELATIONSHIP

Sometimes in a relationship, we love our partner more than they love us, or we love ourselves. This can be challenging. Hugs, love and reciprocation are very important in a relationship. When you find yourself in a relationship that is not fulfilling, find the nearest exit and run. Run and never look back. Sometimes in relationships we find ourselves not wanting to give up on something that was over a long time ago. Let it go and give yourself the opportunity to find a loving relationship. Also, give the other person the opportunity to find true love. Both of you deserve something better.

1 John 4:19

[19] We love him, because he first loved us.

1 Corinthians 13:4-8

[4] Charity suffereth long, and is kind; charity envieth not; charity vaunteth not itself, is not puffed up, [5] Doth not behave itself unseemly, seeketh not her own, is not easily provoked, thinketh no evil; [6] Rejoiceth not in iniquity,

but rejoiceth in the truth; ⁷ Beareth all things, believeth all things, hopeth all things, endureth all things. ⁸ Charity never faileth: but whether there be prophecies, they shall fail; whether there be tongues, they shall cease; whether there be knowledge, it shall vanish away

1 Corinthians 16:14

¹⁴ Let all your things be done with charity.

1 John 4:8

⁸ He that loveth not knoweth not God; for God is love.

23

PRESS ON

Sometimes, you may have a bad moment, day, month, hour or year. You get the point. However, even though you are in the midst of a storm you must still **press on**. Perseverance will make you a winner _all_ the time. **Press on** through your storm. **Press on** through your pain. **Press on** through the bad diagnosis. Believe in yourself. Believe in the higher power.

Philippians 4:13

[13] I can do all things through Christ which strengtheneth me.

I have been through times when I thought I was not going to make it to the other side. But through prayer and with Gods help, I was able to Press on. Never let the enemy see you sweat. Just Press on.

<u>**Hebrews 11:7**</u>

7 By faith Noah, being warned of God of things not seen as yet, moved with fear, prepared an ark to the saving of his house; by the which he condemned the world, and became heir of the righteousness which is by faith.

24

BARE BONES

This is when you have nothing. No money in the bank, no furniture in your home, no place to live and no steady job. You are at the bare bones in life. They say that when we are down to nothing, this is the best time in your lives because we are starting with a clean slate. If you are in this situation, don't cry. You have the perfect opportunity to recreate your life from scratch. It does not matter how old you are, and your education level is not a factor. Mustard seed faith can get you through _everything!_ This is a time in your life when you have to truly believe that things are going to turn around. Pray and work to make your life better. I was so embarrassed when I had a "bare bones" moment in my life. I was embarrassed because I had to deal with this moment with my son as a witness. I had a home, but is was completely empty. He went from living with everything and entered a situation where he had nothing.

I have promised myself, that I will not allow us to live in poverty. I have no idea how I am going to achieve this, but with mustard seed faith, I will make it happen. As I am writing this, we have no living room or dining room furniture. However, we do have each other. For the love of Christian (my son), I am determined to make things happen.

<u>**Luke 17:5-6**</u>

⁵ And the apostles said unto the Lord, Increase our faith. ⁶ And the Lord said, If ye had faith as a grain of mustard seed, ye might say unto this sycamine tree, Be thou plucked up by the root, and be thou planted in the sea; and it should obey you.

<u>**1 Timothy 6:10**</u>

¹⁰ For the love of money is the root of all evil: which while some coveted after, they have erred from the faith, and pierced themselves through with many sorrows.

25

SELF-PRIDE

This is when you love yourself "as is", but you do the necessary work to take care of the temple you were given to live in. Our bodies have the power to heal themselves. However, they have trouble achieving this when we don't take care of ourselves. You have to make sure to drink water, limit your sugar intake and fuel your body with the right nutrients, vitamins and food it needs in order to live your best life possible. Take care of your temple because you only get one.

Proverbs 16:18

[18] Pride goeth before destruction, and an haughty spirit before a fall.

Proverbs 11:2

[2] When pride cometh, then cometh shame: but with the lowly is wisdom.

Love yourself, and all good things will follow. If you have taken a plane flight, you will recall that the attendant told you some safety instructions to follow in the case of an emergency. One important thing they make you aware of is to always put the oxygen mask on yourself first. You can't help another person if you have not taken care of yourself first. Self-pride: take care of yourself, and you will be well equipped to take care of others.

The first person you should fall in love with is **yourself.**

26

STAR, DIRECT AND WRITE

Star, direct and write your own story – they say if you don't stand for something, you'll fall for anything. If you don't write goals and try to achieve these goals you are just coasting through life, and anything and everything can just happen to you. You have to have plans, goals and a definite future written out so that your mind has something to focus on. When you wake up in the morning, you should have goals embedded in your brain that you want to achieve. You are the author and lead actor in your life. Write an award-winning role and win the Oscar. You deserve it. It's your life.

Psalm 25:4-5

4 Shew me thy ways, O Lord; teach me thy paths.
5 Lead me in thy truth, and teach me: for thou art the God of my salvation; on thee do I wait all the day.

James 1:5

5 If any of you lack wisdom, let him ask of God, that giveth to all men liberally, and upbraideth not; and it shall be given him.

<u>**Exodus 33:12-16**</u>

12 And Moses said unto the Lord, See, thou sayest unto me, Bring up this people: and thou hast not let me know whom thou wilt send with me. Yet thou hast said, I know thee by name, and thou hast also found grace in my sight. 13 Now therefore, I pray thee, if I have found grace in thy sight, shew me now thy way, that I may know thee, that I may find grace in thy sight: and consider that this nation is thy people. 14 And he said, My presence shall go with thee, and I will give thee rest. 15 And he said unto him, If thy presence go not with me, carry us not up hence. 16 For wherein shall it be known here that I and thy people have found grace in thy sight? is it not in that thou goest with us? so shall we be separated, I and thy people, from all the people that are upon the face of the earth.

27

SELF-WORTH BUILDING

Whatever you need to do to build up your self-esteem – do it. Sometimes we spend too much time comparing ourselves to others. This can lead us down a wicked path of destruction. Being physically fit can do wonders for the mind, body and soul. Find time in your life to exercise. It is well worth the time. The benefits you receive are tenfold and you will never regret it. Start out with 10 minutes a day and increase this as you go along. Read every day of your life. Read a book, magazine, newspaper article. Read fun stuff, self-help books and things that are going to improve your life. Do things that fill up your cup of life. Let your cup of life overflow with love, peace, happiness and grace.

Things you should practice to build your self-worth:

- Meditation
- Exercise
- Pray
- Start a journal
- Write down your goals and do some work every day that helps you achieve them.
- Practice loving all of those around you and everyone you encounter.

<u>**Psalm 139:13-14**</u>

[13] For thou hast possessed my reins: thou hast covered me in my mother's womb. [14] I will praise thee; for I am fearfully and wonderfully made: marvellous are thy works; and that my soul knoweth right well.

<u>**Genesis 1:26-27**</u>

[26] And God said, Let us make man in our image, after our likeness: and let them have dominion over the fish of the sea, and over the fowl of the air, and over the cattle, and over all the earth, and over every creeping thing that creepeth upon the earth. [27] So God created man in his own image, in the image of God created he him; male and female created he them.

28

REVERSE THE SCRIPT

These are people who know they are wrong, but want to drive you crazy by saying it's you. Never question yourself. Your instincts are correct. They are trying to bamboozle you. Don't fall for the nonsense. Let them know that they are the crazy one, that you won't have it; and reverse the script back to them. Hold them responsible for their mess/messiness.

Some examples of reversing the script:

- Co-workers who try to blame you for something they did.
- Your spouse is cheating, but they try to pretend that it's your fault or you are the one that is cheating.

Revelation 21:8

[8] But the fearful, and unbelieving, and the abominable, and murderers, and whoremongers, and sorcerers, and idolaters, and all liars, shall have their part in the lake which burneth with fire and brimstone: which is the second death.

29

ACCEPT NOTHING

Sometimes, because of our financial circumstances, low self-esteem, family pressure, friends, co-workers or our boss, we tend to go against our own instincts. Accept nothing that will make your heart unhappy. Follow your gut and don't do things that do not feel good to you. You are the creator, author and star in your life. Stand your ground and don't get off course just to please people. You can handle this, and you are more than capable of living your best life for you. Believe in yourself. Trust your instincts and wait for what is right for you to come your way. Get another job if you have to, but don't stay in a bad situation for money. Trust in God and your inner thoughts. Accept trash from no one, no matter what the situation appears to be.

Philippians 4:13

13 I can do all things through Christ which strengtheneth me.

Proverbs 3:1-6

1 My son, forget not my law; but let thine heart keep my commandments: 2 For length of days,

and long life, and peace, shall they add to thee.
³ Let not mercy and truth forsake thee: bind them about thy neck; write them upon the table of thine heart: ⁴ So shalt thou find favour and good understanding in the sight of God and man. ⁵ Trust in the LORD with all thine heart; and lean not unto thine own understanding. ⁶ In all thy ways acknowledge him, and he shall direct thy paths.

30

BE FLEXIBLE

Don't be stubborn and expect everything to go your way. This may sound like a contradiction to Accept Nothing, however it is not. For example, being flexible means allowing the group to decide where to eat dinner tonight, what movie to see, to go skating versus bowling – just roll with the majority, no matter how you feel. Whenever you can be flexible with the group – do it! Just never be flexible when it comes to decisions that affect something major in your life. In that case *stand your ground.*

Romans 12:2

² Ye know that ye were Gentiles, carried away unto these dumb idols, even as ye were led.

1 Corinthians 2:16

¹⁶ For who hath known the mind of the Lord, that he may instruct him? but we have the mind of Christ.

<u>**Ephesians 4:20-24**</u>

[20] But ye have not so learned Christ; [21] If so be that ye have heard him, and have been taught by him, as the truth is in Jesus: [22] That ye put off concerning the former conversation the old man, which is corrupt according to the deceitful lusts; [23] And be renewed in the spirit of your mind; [24] And that ye put on the new man, which after God is created in righteousness and true holiness.

31

JUMP OFF THE TRAIN

Sometimes we are in a relationship or a job, and we are too focused on making it work. There are times when, no matter how hard you try, the relationship, job and situation is dead. Jump off the train before it crashes and burns. You deserve happiness, and happiness is out there waiting for you. Look for it and believe you can have it, and the universe will provide it for you. Don't stay in a job that is killing you internally, or a relationship that is not feeding your soul. You deserve better, and better can only come when you let go and seek it.

<u>Romans 8:28</u>

28 And we know that all things work together for good to them that love God, to them who are the called according to his purpose.

<u>James 4:7</u>

7 But the end of all things is at hand: be ye therefore sober, and watch unto prayer.

32

MOVING PARTS

Understand that life has a basket of surprises for you. Embrace the ones that need embracing, learn from the ones that bring you pain, recognize the ones that are distracting you from your destiny, understand the things that will forever be a part of your life, and proceed with caution. Juggle the parts as you see fit. They do not have to stay where you initially placed them. This year, someone can be a number one priority in your life, and the next year they can be a non-factor in your life. You may need to burn some parts of your life in the fire. Have a clear mindset so that you can always tell the difference between the good and the bad parts – and juggle them accordingly.

<u>James 1:17</u>

[17] Every good gift and every perfect gift is from above, and cometh down from the Father of lights, with whom is no variableness, neither shadow of turning.

<u>**Romans 12:1-2**</u>

[1] I beseech you therefore, brethren, by the mercies of God, that ye present your bodies a living sacrifice, holy, acceptable unto God, which is your reasonable service. [2] And be not conformed to this world: but be ye transformed by the renewing of your mind, that ye may prove what is that good, and acceptable, and perfect, will of God.

33

RETREAT, RELAX, RELATE

I went through a situation where I allowed myself to become badly stressed. I worked myself up over the situation before I knew the outcome. I was tense, overeating, crying and losing all control of my senses. The doctor told me to step back, retreat in my own home and just relax, relate and breathe. I had to learn to find my calmness. Trust me, when you stress yourself out, the outcome will definitely not change – it may even be worse. No good thoughts, outcomes or decision are birthed out of stress. The mind is a powerful thing when you relax; the mind can speak to you and calm your soul, letting you know that everything is going to be alright. So, just calm down and take care of your mind, body and soul.

Philippians 4:6-7

[6] Be careful for nothing; but in every thing by prayer and supplication with thanksgiving let your requests be made known unto God. [7] And the peace of God, which passeth all understanding, shall keep your hearts and minds through Christ Jesus.

34

INSIDE FORGIVENESS

Sometimes, the real problem is that we did not forgive ourselves. We are running amok, acting crazy and blaming everyone else for the things we feel are going wrong in our life. In reality, we are practicing self-sabotage. Until you sit down and forgive yourself for not going to school, following your dreams, and past mistakes, you will continue having the same habitual, damaging behaviors. Let it go so that you move towards having a blissful life.

1 John 1:9-10

[9] If we confess our sins, he is faithful and just to forgive us our sins, and to cleanse us from all unrighteousness. [10] If we say that we have not sinned, we make him a liar, and his word is not in us.

35

PEACE PRAYER

Pray to the God you know or the higher power that you believe in. Sometimes, you find yourself going through a long storm, and you just need to beg for mercy. Pray to God for peace and forgiveness. He will hear your prayer and grant your wish. There were times in my life when I had to ask God for total peace. Peace in my home life, work life, friendships and overall peace. When you are totally overwhelmed and not sure what else to do, just drop down on your knees and pray for peace. God will hear your cry and answer your prayers.

John 14:27

27 Peace I leave with you, my peace I give unto you: not as the world giveth, give I unto you. Let not your heart be troubled, neither let it be afraid.

John 16:33

33 These things I have spoken unto you, that in me ye might have peace. In the world ye shall

have tribulation: but be of good cheer; I have overcome the world.

<u>Hebrews 12:14</u>

14 Follow peace with all men, and holiness, without which no man shall see the Lord:

36

TOTAL EXTERNAL FORGIVENESS

They say that forgiveness is for yourself and not the other person. There were people in my life that I felt had wronged me, and I was so angry at them, I could spit fire all day long. It was not until I learned that forgiveness is always a gift to one's self. Whether you need to forgive yourself or another person, the benefit will always come back to you. Practice forgiveness, and your soul will smile at you every time and every day.

<u>Ephesians 4:32</u>

[32] And be ye kind one to another, tenderhearted, forgiving one another, even as God for Christ's sake hath forgiven you.

<u>John 3:16</u>

[16] For God so loved the world, that he gave his only begotten Son, that whosoever believeth in him should not perish, but have everlasting life.

1 John 1:9

[9] If we confess our sins, he is faithful and just to forgive us our sins, and to cleanse us from all unrighteousness.

2 Corinthians 5:17-18

[17] Therefore if any man be in Christ, he is a new creature: old things are passed away; behold, all things are become new. [18] And all things are of God, who hath reconciled us to himself by Jesus Christ, and hath given to us the ministry of reconciliation;

37

EXPERIENCE LIFE/LIFE EXPERIENCE

Sometimes we let fear direct every course of our life. You have to face the fear and do it anyway. I feared writing this book, feared being a single mom, feared letting my voice be heard. I decided late in life to release my fears and just go for it. That's is why you are reading this book. I read the book *Millionaire Success Habits* by Dean Graziosi, who wrote that he was not the best writer in the world. In spite of that, he wrote his book anyway. This encouraged me to go ahead and write my book. I was never the best student, academically. I started my post academic career at Middlesex County College and had to take a full year of remedial classes before I could begin regular college courses. I just did it, and so can you. Never let anything stop you from experiencing life. You've got this – and you are worth it.

1 Thessalonians 5:16-18

[16] Rejoice evermore. [17] Pray without ceasing. [18] In everything give thanks: for this is the will of God in Christ Jesus concerning you.

John 16:24

²⁴ Hitherto have ye asked nothing in my name: ask, and ye shall receive, that your joy may be full.

1 Peter 1:8

⁸ Whom having not seen, ye love; in whom, though now ye see him not, yet believing, ye rejoice with joy unspeakable and full of glory:

38

FLIP THE SCRIPT

You, and only you, get to write your life story. If you don't write it someone else will write it for you, and trust me – they will not write a leading role for you. You might get a supporting role, at best. When you find yourself in a bad story, the wrong book, a horrible chapter, or no longer playing the leading role ... flip the script and get back to doing what it is you really want to do.

Luke 10:25-37

25 And, behold, a certain lawyer stood up, and tempted him, saying, Master, what shall I do to inherit eternal life? 26 He said unto him, What is written in the law? how readest thou? 27 And he answering said, Thou shalt love the Lord thy God with all thy heart, and with all thy soul, and with all thy strength, and with all thy mind; and thy neighbour as thyself. 28 And he said unto him, Thou hast answered right: this do, and thou shalt live. 29 But he, willing to justify himself, said unto Jesus, And who is my neighbour? 30 And Jesus answering said,

A certain man went down from Jerusalem to Jericho, and fell among thieves, which stripped him of his raiment, and wounded him, and departed, leaving him half dead. [31] And by chance there came down a certain priest that way: and when he saw him, he passed by on the other side. [32] And likewise a Levite, when he was at the place, came and looked on him, and passed by on the other side. [33] But a certain Samaritan, as he journeyed, came where he was: and when he saw him, he had compassion on him, [34] And went to him, and bound up his wounds, pouring in oil and wine, and set him on his own beast, and brought him to an inn, and took care of him. [35] And on the morrow when he departed, he took out two pence, and gave them to the host, and said unto him, Take care of him; and whatsoever thou spendest more, when I come again, I will repay thee. [36] Which now of these three, thinkest thou, was neighbour unto him that fell among the thieves? [37] And he said, He that shewed mercy on him. Then said Jesus unto him, Go, and do thou likewise.

Matthew 6:24

[24] No man can serve two masters: for either he will hate the one, and love the other; or else he will hold to the one, and despise the other. Ye cannot serve God and mammon.

<u>**Psalm 23:1-6**</u>

[1] The Lord is my shepherd; I shall not want.
[2] He maketh me to lie down in green pastures:
he leadeth me beside the still waters. [3] He
restoreth my soul: he leadeth me in the paths of
righteousness for his name's sake. [4] Yea, though I
walk through the valley of the shadow of death,
I will fear no evil: for thou art with me; thy rod
and thy staff they comfort me. [5] Thou preparest a
table before me in the presence of mine enemies:
thou anointest my head with oil; my cup runneth
over. [6] Surely goodness and mercy shall follow me
all the days of my life: and I will dwell in the
house of the Lord for ever.

39

CONCEITED SELF-TALK

Sometimes, you have to look in the mirror and boost yourself up even when you don't feel like it. Trick your mind into believing that you are totally okay with yourself as you are. Practice this every day. At first, it will seem stupid, ridiculous and pointless. However, after doing this for 30 days straight, you will start to believe in yourself more. Believing in yourself, prepares you to conquer the world.

Matthew 11:28-30

28 Come unto me, all ye that labour and are heavy laden, and I will give you rest. 29 Take my yoke upon you, and learn of me; for I am meek and lowly in heart: and ye shall find rest unto your souls. 30 For my yoke is easy, and my burden is light.

40

WRITE IT OUT

The experts say there is something about seeing your plans written out on a piece of paper that helps you bring them to life. Write down your goals and dreams. Write out every single detail. Dedicate at least 10 minutes a day to work on things that support your dreams. One day, out of nowhere, you will see all of your dreams come true.

Habakkuk 2:2

2 And the LORD answered me, and said, Write the vision, and make it plain upon tables, that he may run that readeth it.

Jeremiah 30:2

2 Son of man, prophesy and say, Thus saith the Lord GOD; Howl ye, Woe worth the day!

Deuteronomy 31:19

19 Now therefore write ye this song for you, and teach it the children of Israel: put it in their

mouths, that this song may be a witness for me against the children of Israel.

<u>Revelation 21:1-8</u>

[1] And I saw a new heaven and a new earth: for the first heaven and the first earth were passed away; and there was no more sea. [2] And I John saw the holy city, new Jerusalem, coming down from God out of heaven, prepared as a bride adorned for her husband. [3] And I heard a great voice out of heaven saying, Behold, the tabernacle of God is with men, and he will dwell with them, and they shall be his people, and God himself shall be with them, and be their God. [4] And God shall wipe away all tears from their eyes; and there shall be no more death, neither sorrow, nor crying, neither shall there be any more pain: for the former things are passed away. [5] And he that sat upon the throne said, Behold, I make all things new. And he said unto me, Write: for these words are true and faithful. [6] And he said unto me, It is done. I am Alpha and Omega, the beginning and the end. I will give unto him that is athirst of the fountain of the water of life freely. [7] He that overcometh shall inherit all things; and I will be his God, and he shall be my son. [8] But the fearful, and unbelieving, and the abominable, and murderers, and whoremongers, and sorcerers, and idolaters, and all liars, shall have their part in the lake which burneth with fire and brimstone: which is the second death.

41

LIVE WITHOUT REGRETS

Don't regret the things that you do. Life is to be lived and experienced. Go to the dance, have fun on the date, step outside your comfort zone, and just do what makes your heart feel happy. You are not here to please other people. True happiness comes when you please yourself.

2 Corinthians 7:10

10 For godly sorrow worketh repentance to salvation not to be repented of: but the sorrow of the world worketh death.

Philippians 3:13-15

13 Brethren, I count not myself to have apprehended: but this one thing I do, forgetting those things which are behind, and reaching forth unto those things which are before, 14 I press toward the mark for the prize of the high calling of God in Christ Jesus. 15 Let us therefore,

as many as be perfect, be thus minded: and if
in any thing ye be otherwise minded, God shall
reveal even this unto you.

42

BEST BODY/BODY MAINTENANCE

We all know that exercise is the key to the fountain of youth. The benefits of exercise are immense. Regular exercise can improve your overall mood, protect you from heart disease and a host of other ailments. However, you should also add a healthy diet to your exercise regime. You will thank yourself later when you are in a routine of fueling your mind, body and soul with the right nutrients and exercise. You will think more clearly, and this will provide you with the tools you need to conquer the world.

1 Corinthians 6:12-20

[12] All things are lawful unto me, but all things are not expedient: all things are lawful for me, but I will not be brought under the power of any. [13] Meats for the belly, and the belly for meats: but God shall destroy both it and them. Now the body is not for fornication, but for the Lord; and the Lord for the body. [14] And God hath both raised up the Lord, and will also raise up us by his own power. [15] Know ye not that your bodies are the members of Christ? shall I then take the

members of Christ, and make them the members of an harlot? God forbid. [16] What? know ye not that he which is joined to an harlot is one body? for two, saith he, shall be one flesh. [17] But he that is joined unto the Lord is one spirit. [18] Flee fornication. Every sin that a man doeth is without the body; but he that committeth fornication sinneth against his own body. [19] What? know ye not that your body is the temple of the Holy Ghost which is in you, which ye have of God, and ye are not your own? [20] For ye are bought with a price: therefore glorify God in your body, and in your spirit, which are God's.

43

VIRTUAL SUPPORT

Trying to comfort someone over the phone, via skype or text can be a challenge. Sometimes, it is easier, in person, to just give a hug and not say a word. Body language, eye contact, or the touch of a hand can be so reassuring when someone needs you. However, we are living in the text/social media and high-tech age. In a pinch, the best way we can connect with people is via social media, FaceTime and/or over the phone. Tell them you would be there in person, if you could. Talk with compassion. Stay on the line with them as long as they need you. I have fallen asleep with people I love, while on the phone. We laughed about it the next day. Always support a friend in need, even if it is virtual.

Matthew 6:5-13

5 And when thou prayest, thou shalt not be as the hypocrites are: for they love to pray standing in the synagogues and in the corners of the streets, that they may be seen of men. Verily I say unto you, They have their reward. 6 But thou, when thou prayest, enter into thy closet, and when thou hast shut thy door, pray to thy Father which

is in secret; and thy Father which seeth in secret shall reward thee openly. [7] But when ye pray, use not vain repetitions, as the heathen do: for they think that they shall be heard for their much speaking. [8] Be not ye therefore like unto them: for your Father knoweth what things ye have need of, before ye ask him. [9] After this manner therefore pray ye: Our Father which art in heaven, Hallowed be thy name. [10] Thy kingdom come, Thy will be done in earth, as it is in heaven. [11] Give us this day our daily bread. [12] And forgive us our debts, as we forgive our debtors. [13] And lead us not into temptation, but deliver us from evil: For thine is the kingdom, and the power, and the glory, for ever. Amen.

44

SELF-EDUCATION

Education that yields a degree of some sort is a wonderful thing. I would never tell anyone not to study for a degree. I have several. However, the best education is self-education. I am a book store lover. I live in the self-help section. If you don't have a degree, don't let that hold you back. Here are a few people that were very successful and did not have a degree;

- **Abraham Lincoln**, was a self-educated lawyer and United States president. He finished one year of formal schooling, taught himself higher level math, and read Blackstone on his own to become a lawyer.
- **Andrew Carnegie,** industrialist and philanthropist, and he was one of the first multi-billionaires in the United States of America. He was an elementary school dropout and was still successful.
- **Andrew Jackson**, was a United States president, general, attorney, judge and congressman. He was home-schooled. However, he became a practicing attorney by the age of 35, all of this without a formal school education.
- **Bob Proctor**, motivational speaker, bestselling author, and co-founder of Life Success Publishing, a very successful

business. It is reported he only attended two months of high school.

- **Coco Chanel**, founder of famous fashion brand, Chanel, which I absolutely love. She has a perfume bearing her name, Chanel No. 5. This perfume has kept her name famous tp this day. Coco Chanel was self-taught.
- **Dave Thomas**, is the billionaire founder of Wendy's. He dropped out of high school at tender age of 15.
- **Henry Ford**, is the billionaire founder of Ford Motor Company. He did not attend college.
- **Rachael Ray**, is a Food Network cooking show star, and food industry entrepreneur, with no formal culinary arts training. She never attended college.
- **Simon Cowell**, is a TV producer and music judge on American Idol, The X Factor and Britain's Got Talent. He is a high school dropout.
- **Walt Disney**, the founder of the Walt Disney Company. He dropped out of high school at tender age of 16.

I am by no means telling you to drop out of school, or not attend college. I am just letting you know that a mixture of formal and self-education can take you to the moon and back.

Psalm 41:1-13

[1] Now it came to pass in the seventh month, that Ishmael the son of Nethaniah the son of Elishama, of the seed royal, and the princes of the king, even ten men with him, came unto Gedaliah the son of Ahikam to Mizpah; and there they did eat bread together in Mizpah. [2] Then arose Ishmael the son of Nethaniah, and the ten men that were with him, and smote Gedaliah the son of Ahikam the

son of Shaphan with the sword, and slew him, whom the king of Babylon had made governor over the land. ³ Ishmael also slew all the Jews that were with him, even with Gedaliah, at Mizpah, and the Chaldeans that were found there, and the men of war. ⁴ And it came to pass the second day after he had slain Gedaliah, and no man knew it, ⁵ That there came certain from Shechem, from Shiloh, and from Samaria, even fourscore men, having their beards shaven, and their clothes rent, and having cut themselves, with offerings and incense in their hand, to bring them to the house of the LORD. ⁶ And Ishmael the son of Nethaniah went forth from Mizpah to meet them, weeping all along as he went: and it came to pass, as he met them, he said unto them, Come to Gedaliah the son of Ahikam. ⁷ And it was so, when they came into the midst of the city, that Ishmael the son of Nethaniah slew them, and cast them into the midst of the pit, he, and the men that were with him. ⁸ But ten men were found among them that said unto Ishmael, Slay us not: for we have treasures in the field, of wheat, and of barley, and of oil, and of honey. So he forbare, and slew them not among their brethren. ⁹ Now the pit wherein Ishmael had cast all the dead bodies of the men, whom he had slain because of Gedaliah, was it which Asa the king had made for fear of Baasha king of Israel: and Ishmael the son of Nethaniah filled it with them that were slain. ¹⁰ Then Ishmael carried away captive all the residue of the people that were in Mizpah, even the king's daughters, and all the people that remained in

Mizpah, whom Nebuzaradan the captain of the guard had committed to Gedaliah the son of Ahikam: and Ishmael the son of Nethaniah carried them away captive, and departed to go over to the Ammonites. [11] But when Johanan the son of Kareah, and all the captains of the forces that were with him, heard of all the evil that Ishmael the son of Nethaniah had done, [12] Then they took all the men, and went to fight with Ishmael the son of Nethaniah, and found him by the great waters that are in Gibeon. [13] Now it came to pass, that when all the people which were with Ishmael saw Johanan the son of Kareah, and all the captains of the forces that were with him, then they were glad.

45

IMPRISONED MINDSET

This is when you are stuck in a routine. You are not open to new ideas or different ways of doing things, and you refuse to think outside the box. You are rigid and living life in a vicious cycle of nothingness. Free your mind and live your life. I know that it sounds simple, but how do you go about actually doing this? You can start by reading some self-help books. I love Wayne Dyer, who completely changed my life. His work is amazing and he left us with some amazing gifts; any one of his books will be a good start. Prayer, meditation and exercise, as I stated before, will also help you clear your mind. Most importantly, you need to start with one goal that you want to achieve within the next 30 days.

The goal should be reasonable, attainable and you have to write it down. It would help if you can get an accountability partner; someone you have to answer to in order to keep you on track with your goal. Once you achieve one goal you will be on the road to changing your imprisoned mindset and working towards achieving more and more goals.

Matthew 25:36

36 Naked, and ye clothed me: I was sick, and ye visited me: I was in prison, and ye came unto me.

Isaiah 61:1

¹ The Spirit of the Lord GOD is upon me; because the LORD hath anointed me to preach good tidings unto the meek; he hath sent me to bind up the brokenhearted, to proclaim liberty to the captives, and the opening of the prison to them that are bound;

Hebrews 13:3

³ Remember them that are in bonds, as bound with them; and them which suffer adversity, as being yourselves also in the body.

Ezra 7:26

²⁶ And whosoever will not do the law of thy God, and the law of the king, let judgment be executed speedily upon him, whether it be unto death, or to banishment, or to confiscation of goods, or to imprisonment.

46

DELAYED TALENT

This is when you know you have a clear, defined talent, like singing, dancing, writing, etc. Instead of cultivating your talent, you are distracting yourself by doing something that has nothing to do with your talent. You are miserable and will stay that way until you follow your bliss. Some of us spend a lifetime trying to figure out what we want to do with our life. Others clearly have a natural-born talent and let doubt, disappointment and low self-esteem keep them from following their bliss. Delayed talent can be turned into actualized or realized talent the minute you decide to do something different. Decide today to do something different and turn your life around.

1 Peter 4:10-11

[10] As every man hath received the gift, even so minister the same one to another, as good stewards of the manifold grace of God. [11] If any man speak, let him speak as the oracles of God; if any man minister, let him do it as of the ability which God giveth: that God in all things may be glorified through Jesus Christ, to whom be praise and dominion for ever and ever. Amen.

47

SURRENDER EVERYTHING

Give up everything in order to find yourself and live your dream life. Sometimes you have to surrender the idea of where you thought your life would be at a certain point. Live in the now, because that is all you truly have. Some people beat themselves up over and over again. They live in this vicious cycle of blame, regret, self-doubt and would-have, could-have, should-have. This is the enemy trying to steal your current joy, as it has stolen your past joy. It is up to you to see and stop the plan of the enemy. Pray and surrender everything. Once you pray, move forward and achieve your dreams.

John 15:1-7

¹ I am the true vine, and my Father is the husbandman. ² Every branch in me that beareth not fruit he taketh away: and every branch that beareth fruit, he purgeth it, that it may bring forth more fruit. ³ Now ye are clean through the word which I have spoken unto you .⁴ Abide in me, and I in you. As the branch cannot bear fruit of itself, except it abide in the vine; no more can ye, except ye abide in me. ⁵ I am the vine, ye are

the branches: He that abideth in me, and I in him, the same bringeth forth much fruit: for without me ye can do nothing. [6] If a man abide not in me, he is cast forth as a branch, and is withered; and men gather them, and cast them into the fire, and they are burned. [7] If ye abide in me, and my words abide in you, ye shall ask what ye will, and it shall be done unto you.

James 4:7

[7] Submit yourselves therefore to God. Resist the devil, and he will flee from you.

48

BUDGET FRIENDLY

Live within your means. So, what exactly does this mean? To live within your means comprises of you spending less than or equal to the amount you earn each month. The caveat is that the amount you spend must include paying all of your bills and living expenses for the month. This is a difficult task for most people. However, there are people out there achieving it, and so can you. The plastic/credit card world allows people to purchase more than they can afford, month after month. In addition, loans, savings and even emergency funds allow you to buy more things than your income would allow. So, how do you resist the urge to live beyond your means? Take a 30-day break; you owe it to yourself, and just use _cash_ to purchase _all_ the things you want within those 30 days. You will notice that you will not be able to buy everything you see and want. You will also notice that this does not leave you as empty as you thought it would. You want to live a budget-friendly life. This will bring you more happiness than you could ever imagine.

<u>Proverbs 13:22</u>

22 A good man leaveth an inheritance to his children's children: and the wealth of the sinner is laid up for the just.

<u>**Matthew 6:24**</u>

[24] No man can serve two masters: for either he will hate the one, and love the other; or else he will hold to the one, and despise the other. Ye cannot serve God and mammon.

49

NIGHTTIME CRY

This is when you are going through a rough time in your life, you just feel like crying, day and night. Life happens and most of us can't afford to lose our day job because of our trials and tribulations. My advice: get through your workday and cry at night when you get home. Sometimes, we are going through so much we feel like crying all day long. Reserve your tears for the nighttime. Don't let any situation stop you from making your "bag".

The Bible states in **Psalm 30:5:** For his anger endured but a moment; in his favor is life: weeping may endure for a **night**, but joy cometh in the **morning**.

Revelation 21:1-4

[1] And I saw a new heaven and a new earth: for the first heaven and the first earth were passed away; and there was no more sea. [2] And I John saw the holy city, new Jerusalem, coming down from God out of heaven, prepared as a bride adorned for her husband. [3] And I heard a great voice out of heaven saying, Behold, the tabernacle of God is with men, and he will dwell with them, and

they shall be his people, and God himself shall be with them, and be their God. ⁴ And God shall wipe away all tears from their eyes; and there shall be no more death, neither sorrow, nor crying, neither shall there be any more pain: for the former things are passed away.

50

BOTTLED EMOTIONS

This happens when you don't express your emotions and you just keep them inside and allow them to explode at the wrong time. This is what we call bottled emotions. Every night before you go to bed, release all the negative feelings and emotions that occurred throughout the day. Shout it out when you are by yourself in the room. Talk to yourself in the mirror. Pretend you are talking to the person you feel has wronged you. Just let go of it each night, so that you won't take it into the next day. Also, you don't want the negativity to disrupt your sleep. I try to practice giving all my negative emotions to God for resolution before I go to bed. Most of the time you will not be able to resolve situations on your own. Why not hand it over to the one that can help you? When you release bottled emotions, they don't have time to fester within you and wreak havoc. Stress and bad emotions can wreak havoc on your body, and cause disease. To live your best life, you have to keep your body and mental health in the best condition possible. So, if something is bothering you, trash it and move on. Speak to the person that wronged you, and move on. If it is your current job, do the best you can and move on as soon as you can.

Romans 8:28

28 And we know that all things work together for good to them that love God, to them who are the called according to his purpose.

Galatians 5:16-24

16 This I say then, Walk in the Spirit, and ye shall not fulfil the lust of the flesh. **17** For the flesh lusteth against the Spirit, and the Spirit against the flesh: and these are contrary the one to the other: so that ye cannot do the things that ye would. **18** But if ye be led of the Spirit, ye are not under the law. **19** Now the works of the flesh are manifest, which are these; Adultery, fornication, uncleanness, lasciviousness, **20** Idolatry, witchcraft, hatred, variance, emulations, wrath, strife, seditions, heresies, **21** Envyings, murders, drunkenness, revellings, and such like: of the which I tell you before, as I have also told you in time past, that they which do such things shall not inherit the kingdom of God. **22** But the fruit of the Spirit is love, joy, peace, longsuffering, gentleness, goodness, faith, **23** Meekness, temperance: against such there is no law. **24** And they that are Christ's have crucified the flesh with the affections and lusts.

51

TIMED RESPONSE

Think before you speak. I grew up in the era when children would say, "sticks and stones can break my bones, but words will never hurt me." Well, that statement is false. Words hurt – and they can penetrate the mind, body and soul. When you are angry, practice silence. When happy, release your silence and use your words. It's also important to learn how to apologize less. What are you talking about, lady? If you don't have loose lips, you can hear the person communicating with you. Truly listening it might change your response. When in doubt, err on the side of kindness. You will be thankful later, and so will the receiver. Watch your tongue and mind your mouth. When you are angry, wait 15 minutes before speaking. If, in 15 minutes, you are still pissed, wait another 15 minutes. My point is, don't open your mouth and use your words until you have calmed down.

Romans 8:28

[28] And we know that all things work together for good to them that love God, to them who are the called according to his purpose.

<u>**Philippians 4:13**</u>

[13] I can do all things through Christ which strengtheneth me.

52

FORCED SOLITUDE

Sometimes, we go through storms in our life that force us to make a complete U-turn. We are forced to retreat from our current ways of thinking, listening and doing. When you have no other option in life, always, and I mean _always_, believe in yourself. Meditate, pray, exercise and give yourself an opportunity to hear the voices within, and listen to your gut feeling. We can recover from pain if we give ourselves a minute to have a moment of silence. Force yourself to be with yourself in order to find the person you lost along the way. This does not mean that you should isolate yourself from people _forever_. It just means that sometimes you have to take a step back and refill your cup, which may be only 10 percent full. You need to stay in a constant flow of overflow. That way when someone needs help, you can help them without depleting yourself.

Matthew 6:6

6 But thou, when thou prayest, enter into thy closet, and when thou hast shut thy door, pray to thy Father which is in secret; and thy Father which seeth in secret shall reward thee openly.

Luke 5:15-16

¹⁵ But so much the more went there a fame abroad of him: and great multitudes came together to hear, and to be healed by him of their infirmities. ¹⁶ And he withdrew himself into the wilderness, and prayed.

Luke 6:12

¹² And it came to pass in those days, that he went out into a mountain to pray, and continued all night in prayer to God.

Mark 6:31

³¹ And he said unto them, Come ye yourselves apart into a desert place, and rest a while: for there were many coming and going, and they had no leisure so much as to eat.

Matthew 6:1-4

1 Take heed that ye do not your alms before men, to be seen of them: otherwise ye have no reward of your Father which is in heaven. ² Therefore when thou doest thine alms, do not sound a trumpet before thee, as the hypocrites do in the synagogues and in the streets, that they may have glory of men. Verily I say unto you, They have their reward. ³ But when thou doest alms, let not thy left hand know what thy right hand doeth: ⁴ That thine alms may be in secret: and thy Father which seeth in secret himself shall reward thee openly.

53

YOUR BEST BODY

Never stop trying to be in the best shape of your life. I own more than a dozen exercise DVDs, a plethora of fitness books, and I have purchased my fair share of health magazines. Whether by osmosis or simply just pure frustration of being stuck in a rut, I will utilize all of the materials I have one day to live in my best body. Never give up on yourself. Find a partner, or be your own partner, but give yourself a fighting chance. Exercise is the best medicine and will care for *all* of your woes.

Endorphins are produced in your body in various stressful situations, and a group of hormones are secreted throughout the brain and body during intense stress (which we want to avoid) or arousal, and are part of the "fight-or-flight" response. Endorphins do very good things for your body. They can relieve pain, produce feelings of pleasure, reduce stress, and increase relaxation. The best way to stimulate the release of endorphins is through exercise. So do some yoga, take a walk or actually start using that gym membership I know you have. Produce some good endorphins and enjoy **your best body**.

1 Corinthians 6:12-20

Stay Away from Sexual Sin

[12] All things are lawful unto me, but all things are not expedient: all things are lawful for me, but I will not be brought under the power of any. [13] Meats for the belly, and the belly for meats: but God shall destroy both it and them. Now the body is not for fornication, but for the Lord; and the Lord for the body. [14] And God hath both raised up the Lord, and will also raise up us by his own power. [15] Know ye not that your bodies are the members of Christ? shall I then take the members of Christ, and make them the members of an harlot? God forbid. [16] What? know ye not that he which is joined to an harlot is one body? for two, saith he, shall be one flesh. [17] But he that is joined unto the Lord is one spirit. [18] Flee fornication. Every sin that a man doeth is without the body; but he that committeth fornication sinneth against his own body. [19] What? know ye not that your body is the temple of the Holy Ghost which is in you, which ye have of God, and ye are not your own? [20] For ye are bought with a price: therefore glorify God in your body, and in your spirit, which are God's.

54

SURVIVAL MOMENT

My survival moment came after God completely broke me down, and on bended knee, with his help, I had to build myself back up. Sometimes, bad relationships, mismatched employment situations, unemployment and a host of other life situations take us down a road we don't want to go. The road is dark, lonely, heart-wrenching and completely debilitating. At some point you have to slip into your survival moment. If you don't you will find yourself depressed, broken and feeling like you are just not going to make it.

After periods of self-loathing that ranged from minutes, days, months, and even years, I had a breakthrough, and I slipped into a **survival moment** which enabled me to live my best life. Take your setbacks one day at a time. You have the power within you to turn your situation around. All it takes is a mustard seed faith. Work hard to get into your survival moment. It's worth your future to get into your survival moment as quickly as possible.

<u>1 Corinthians 16:13-14</u>

[13] Watch ye, stand fast in the faith, quit you like men, be strong. [14] Let all your things be done with charity.

Joshua 1:9

⁹ Have not I commanded thee? Be strong and of a good courage; be not afraid, neither be thou dismayed: for the LORD thy God is with thee whithersoever thou goest.

Philippians 4:13

¹³ I can do all things through Christ which strengtheneth me.

John 3:16

¹⁶ For God so loved the world, that he gave his only begotten Son, that whosoever believeth in him should not perish, but have everlasting life.

55

ENTREPRENEUR SPIRIT

You have got it in you. Change your life by following your dreams. Be a dream catcher. The best things in life happen when you believe in yourself, follow your bliss and just do what you were meant to do in life. Don't be afraid of going after your dreams. I started to truly live once I believed in myself. You have to take this thing one day at a time. Do a little something every day that will help you towards achieving your life goals. Sometimes you have no choice but to do a day job while working on your dream. Do whatever it is you have to do in order to be successful in your day job and get the bills paid, while working on your dream. Praying makes dreams come true all the time for those who truly believe and work on it.

Matthew 25:14-30

[14] For the kingdom of heaven is as a man travelling into a far country, who called his own servants, and delivered unto them his goods. [15] And unto one he gave five talents, to another two, and to another one; to every man according to his several ability; and straightway took his journey. [16] Then he that had received the five talents went and

traded with the same, and made them other five talents.[17] And likewise he that had received two, he also gained other two.[18] But he that had received one went and digged in the earth, and hid his lord's money.[19] After a long time the lord of those servants cometh, and reckoneth with them.[20] And so he that had received five talents came and brought other five talents, saying, Lord, thou deliveredst unto me five talents: behold, I have gained beside them five talents more.[21] His lord said unto him, Well done, thou good and faithful servant: thou hast been faithful over a few things, I will make thee ruler over many things: enter thou into the joy of thy lord.[22] He also that had received two talents came and said, Lord, thou deliveredst unto me two talents: behold, I have gained two other talents beside them.[23] His lord said unto him, Well done, good and faithful servant; thou hast been faithful over a few things, I will make thee ruler over many things: enter thou into the joy of thy lord.[24] Then he which had received the one talent came and said, Lord, I knew thee that thou art an hard man, reaping where thou hast not sown, and gathering where thou hast not strawed:[25] And I was afraid, and went and hid thy talent in the earth: lo, there thou hast that is thine.[26] His lord answered and said unto him, Thou wicked and slothful servant, thou knewest that I reap where I sowed not, and gather where I have not strawed:[27] Thou oughtest therefore to have put my money to the exchangers, and then at my coming I should have received mine own with usury.[28] Take therefore the talent from him, and give it unto him which hath ten talents.[29] For unto every one that hath shall be given, and he shall have abundance: but from him that hath not shall be taken away even that which he hath.[30] And cast ye the unprofitable servant into outer darkness: there shall be weeping and gnashing of teeth

56

PERFECT SILENCE

This is like meditating. To hear your own thoughts and God within you, you have to practice perfect silence. Cut off the television, shut down the cellphone, and take a break from social media. Your mind needs a break. It needs you to listen. Everything that you need to survive and live your best life is already within you. However, you will not be able to hear it if you don't quiet your mind. Social media has caused the world a huge distraction that we did not need. The only way around this distraction is to practice perfect silence at least 15-20 minutes per day. You owe it to yourself.

Romans 3:23

23 For all have sinned, and come short of the glory of God;

Romans 10:9

9 That if thou shalt confess with thy mouth the Lord Jesus, and shalt believe in thine heart that God hath raised him from the dead, thou shalt be saved.

Romans 10:13

¹³ For whosoever shall call upon the name of the Lord shall be saved.

Proverbs 21:23

²³ Whoso keepeth his mouth and his tongue keepeth his soul from troubles.

Revelation 3:20

²⁰ Behold, I stand at the door, and knock: if any man hear my voice, and open the door, I will come in to him, and will sup with him, and he with me.

57

MOMENTARY SILENCE

Don't speak in haste, but rather address the shenanigans later. Sometimes people try to bait others. They will antagonize you, push every button so that you will fall into the rabbit hole. Just know that there are no carrots waiting for you down in the rabbit hole. So, breathe, take a moment and absorb what they are putting out, but don't let the left hand know what the right hand is doing.

Proverbs 18:13

[13] He that answereth a matter before he heareth it, it is folly and shame unto him.

Ephesians 4:29

[29] Let no corrupt communication proceed out of your mouth, but that which is good to the use of edifying, that it may minister grace unto the hearers.

<u>**Psalm 141:3**</u>

[3] Set a watch, O Lord, before my mouth; keep the door of my lips.

58

DECISION BUDDY

Always have a trustworthy person that you can bounce ideas off. They are the one and only person you should consult when you need a neutral person to help you make a decision. Sometimes, when we are faced with a difficult decision, our thoughts are clouded in fog. Of course, you should always, and I mean *always*, pray to God first. If you still can't sleep, speak to your neutral friend, who will tell you the truth, even if it hurts. By the way: The Higher Power can be your decision buddy. However, if you don't quiet your mind you will not hear His response. Sometimes, God has to get the message through to us via our *trusted decision buddy.* You have to trust this person without a doubt, otherwise it will be a wasted effort to seeking advice from them. Advice from someone you don't trust is a bomb waiting to explode.

John 15:12-15

[12] This is my commandment, That ye love one another, as I have loved you. [13] Greater love hath no man than this, that a man lay down his life for his friends. [14] Ye are my friends, if ye do whatsoever I command you. [15] Henceforth I call

you not servants; for the servant knoweth not
what his lord doeth: but I have called you friends;
for all things that I have heard of my Father I
have made known unto you.

59

MANSION MINDSET

Have a mindset that enables you to always think bigger and better. Create a vision board, and look at it as often as possible – morning, noon and night. Let your good vibes and vision lead you along the way. Sometimes our current circumstances are so bleak, we just can't see our way out. Don't let your current situation lock you in despair. I can't stop referring to mustard seed faith. God can turn any situation around with just a mustard seed faith. You just have to believe and you can achieve.

Hebrews 13:5

[5] Let your conversation be without covetousness; and be content with such things as ye have: for he hath said, I will never leave thee, nor forsake thee.

1 Timothy 6:10

[10] For the love of money is the root of all evil: which while some coveted after, they have erred

from the faith, and pierced themselves through with many sorrows.

<u>Proverbs 13:11</u>

[11] Wealth gotten by vanity shall be diminished: but he that gathereth by labour shall increase.

60

WRITTEN SUCCESS

Write down your life goals and read them every chance you get. There is something powerful in the written word. You can change your life by writing down your goals and following your dreams. Write it out and look at it often, and before you know it you will be living the life of your dreams. You will have to put in some work. You can't just write down, "I want to be a millionaire" and wake up rich a few days later. However, like Benjamin Franklin said, "If you fail to plan, you are planning to fail!" So, write it down and plan to win.

Psalm 37:4-5

[4] Delight thyself also in the Lord: and he shall give thee the desires of thine heart. 5 Commit thy way unto the Lord; trust also in him; and he shall bring it to pass.

Philippians 4:13

[13] I can do all things through Christ which strengtheneth me.

Philippians 3:13-14

13 Brethren, I count not myself to have apprehended: but this one thing I do, forgetting those things which are behind, and reaching forth unto those things which are before, 14 I press toward the mark for the prize of the high calling of God in Christ Jesus.

Proverbs 3:5-6

5 Trust in the LORD with all thine heart; and lean not unto thine own understanding. 6 In all thy ways acknowledge him, and he shall direct thy paths.

61

DOLLAR DAYS

Once a week, spend a dollar on a perfect stranger. Leave a dollar at your favorite coffee shop and tell them to give the next person $1.00 off their drink. Dollar days are so much fun and it won't cost you a lot to make a difference in someone else's life or put a smile on their face. The art of giving is about creating an unconditional and joyful abundance of love, peace and happiness for yourself and others. Your gestures of kindness and generosity will bring you a wealth of contentment.

2 Corinthians 9:13

[13] Whiles by the experiment of this ministration they glorify God for your professed subjection unto the gospel of Christ, and for your liberal distribution unto them, and unto all men;

Hebrews 13:15-16

[15] By him therefore let us offer the sacrifice of praise to God continually, that is, the fruit of our lips giving thanks to his name. [16] But to do good

and to communicate forget not: for with such sacrifices God is well pleased.

<u>Mark 16:15-16</u>

[15] And he said unto them, Go ye into all the world, and preach the gospel to every creature. [16] He that believeth and is baptized shall be saved; but he that believeth not shall be damned.

62

UNRECOGNIZED FORGIVENESS

Check your baggage at the door. Sometimes we move into a new relationship too soon. If you don't forgive yourself and the other person for a pervious relationship gone wrong, you can unknowingly bring that baggage into the new relationship. When that baggage surfaces in the new relationship, it won't be pretty. So how do you let go of the baggage? Through unrecognized forgiveness. When someone apologizes to you face to face, over the phone, via text or the old fashion way via a hand written letter, recognize the apology and decide whether or not you are going to forgive them.

However, there will be times you may have a situation where the apology is never going to happen. Maybe the apology did happen, but it did not happen the way that you wanted it to happen. That is when you must practice **unrecognized forgiveness**. Unrecognized forgiveness means:

- You never received an apology.
- The apology did not turn out how you expected.
- You want to seek revenge on the person for the way they treated you.

But instead, you replay the situation in your mind differently and act as if you received the apology and forgave the transgression. You forgive the transgression in spite of never having received an actual apology.

Matthew 6:9-15

[9] After this manner therefore pray ye: Our Father which art in heaven, Hallowed be thy name. [10] Thy kingdom come, Thy will be done in earth, as it is in heaven. [11] Give us this day our daily bread. [12] And forgive us our debts, as we forgive our debtors. [13] And lead us not into temptation, but deliver us from evil: For thine is the kingdom, and the power, and the glory, for ever. Amen. [14] For if ye forgive men their trespasses, your heavenly Father will also forgive you: [15] But if ye forgive not men their trespasses, neither will your Father forgive your trespasses.

63

UNDELIVERED MAIL

Write a letter to those who have hurt you. You don't even have to give it to them. It's helpful to write it out. Your feelings need a home. When you tell your loved one that you love them, what a great feeling! But when you keep the hurt feeling inside, it can fester and grow into something quite harmful. Instead, just write it out and address it to the person that hurt you, even if you never have a chance to deliver it. Your body needs to release the negative energy. Release it in written form, or it will wreak havoc on your mind, body and soul.

Proverbs 16:7

⁷ When a man's ways please the Lord, he maketh even his enemies to be at peace with him.

Hebrews 12:14

¹⁴ Follow peace with all men, and holiness, without which no man shall see the Lord:

John 16:33

³³ These things I have spoken unto you, that in me ye might have peace. In the world ye shall have tribulation: but be of good cheer; I have overcome the world.

1 Peter 3:9-11

⁹ Not rendering evil for evil, or railing for railing: but contrariwise blessing; knowing that ye are thereunto called, that ye should inherit a blessing. ¹⁰ For he that will love life, and see good days, let him refrain his tongue from evil, and his lips that they speak no guile: ¹¹ Let him eschew evil, and do good; let him seek peace, and ensue it.

64

FAMILY PLANNER

Spend time with your family. Family time is always great. You will get closer to the ones you love and reduce your stress. This means that even if you have to be the one to always get your family together, do what you have to do. Plan a yearly family dinner. Allow, the drunk uncle to attend, the mess-starter, friends and family members that have done you wrong in the past. Even invite the family or friend that owes you money and has never paid it back. This yearly dinner is your redemption meal. You don't have to spend all night with them. This meal should have a time frame. Feed them. Love them and tell them when it is time to go home. We should always forgive family, and food is always a good way to kiss and make up.

1 Corinthians 13:4-8

[4] Charity suffereth long, and is kind; charity envieth not; charity vaunteth not itself, is not puffed up, [5] Doth not behave itself unseemly, seeketh not her own, is not easily provoked, thinketh no evil; [6] Rejoiceth not in iniquity, but rejoiceth in the truth; [7] Beareth all things, believeth all things, hopeth all things, endureth

all things. [8] Charity never faileth: but whether there be prophecies, they shall fail; whether there be tongues, they shall cease; whether there be knowledge, it shall vanish away.

65

CUP OF FULLNESS

Practice gratefulness. Your cup will be full and you will see your life change dramatically when you practice gratefulness daily. Be grateful for your life, the life of your loved ones. Be grateful that you have a job, interview for a job, and even being retired from a job. Be grateful you can see, walk, talk, eat and live your life to the fullest. There is always something to be grateful for, even if you are in the worst of circumstances. An attitude of gratitude will drastically change your life for the better. Try starting a gratefulness journal and have fun seeing how many things you can be grateful for every day.

1 Thessalonians 5:16-18

[16] Rejoice evermore. [17] Pray without ceasing. [18] In every thing give thanks: for this is the will of God in Christ Jesus concerning you.

Psalm 100:1-5

1 Make a joyful noise unto the LORD, all ye lands. [2] Serve the LORD with gladness: come before his presence with singing. [3] Know ye that

the LORD he is God: it is he that hath made us, and not we ourselves; we are his people, and the sheep of his pasture. ⁴ Enter into his gates with thanksgiving, and into his courts with praise: be thankful unto him, and bless his name. ⁵ For the LORD is good; his mercy is everlasting; and his truth endureth to all generations.

Colossians 3:15-20

¹⁵ And let the peace of God rule in your hearts, to the which also ye are called in one body; and be ye thankful. ¹⁶ Let the word of Christ dwell in you richly in all wisdom; teaching and admonishing one another in psalms and hymns and spiritual songs, singing with grace in your hearts to the Lord. ¹⁷ And whatsoever ye do in word or deed, do all in the name of the Lord Jesus, giving thanks to God and the Father by him. ¹⁸ Wives, submit yourselves unto your own husbands, as it is fit in the Lord. ¹⁹ Husbands, love your wives, and be not bitter against them. ²⁰ Children, obey your parents in all things: for this is well pleasing unto the Lord

66

DETERMINED SUCCESS

You determine your success. He who fails to plan, plans to fail. Never give up on your dream. It will come to pass. You just have to work towards it daily. Take small steps every day, and one day you will walk into your destiny. Don't listen to the naysayers. You have to encourage and believe in yourself every single day. Take this process one step at a time. Start by creating your goals and being clear on exactly what is it you want to do with your life. Second, manage your time and productivity by setting a schedule for yourself. If your goal is to be in the best shape you've even been, plan to get up every morning by 5 am and workout for ½ hour in order to achieve that goal. Third, no matter how long it takes maintain a good attitude, don't be disappointed when you see others making it or being more successful than you. Your time will come. Just stick to the plan. Visualize your success, and visualize nothing but being successful. Lastly, you may hit bumps in the road. So, you are going to have to learn how to overcome your failures. Keep trying until you make it – and you _will_ make it.

Proverbs 3:1-4

[1] My son, forget not my law; but let thine heart keep my commandments: [2] For length of days,

and long life, and peace, shall they add to thee.
³ Let not mercy and truth forsake thee: bind them about thy neck; write them upon the table of thine heart: ⁴ So shalt thou find favour and good understanding in the sight of God and man.

Proverbs 16:3

³ Commit thy works unto the Lord, and thy thoughts shall be established.

Psalm 37:4

⁴ Delight thyself also in the Lord: and he shall give thee the desires of thine heart.

James 4:10

¹⁰ Humble yourselves in the sight of the Lord, and he shall lift you up.

Matthew 6:25-26

²⁵ Therefore I say unto you, Take no thought for your life, what ye shall eat, or what ye shall drink; nor yet for your body, what ye shall put on. Is not the life more than meat, and the body than raiment?²⁶ Behold the fowls of the air: for they sow not, neither do they reap, nor gather into barns; yet your heavenly Father feedeth them. Are ye not much better than they?

67

SHARED SECRETS

Tell your deepest secrets only to your significant other or best friend. That's like telling 1,000 people. They will always have someone else they share it with even if you tell them not too. First speak to God and then if you still have the need to tell someone else; talk to one or two people after that, and no one else. You don't want your personal business to be known around town. Sometimes, silence is golden because, for some reason, people just love to talk about other people. Don't be the source of people's gossip.

Luke 8:17

17 For nothing is secret, that shall not be made manifest; neither any thing hid, that shall not be known and come abroad.

Luke 12:3

3 Therefore whatsoever ye have spoken in darkness shall be heard in the light; and that which ye have spoken in the ear in closets shall be proclaimed upon the housetops.

Mark 4:22

22 For there is nothing hid, which shall not be manifested; neither was any thing kept secret, but that it should come abroad.

Ecclesiastes 12:14

14 For God shall bring every work into judgment, with every secret thing, whether it be good, or whether it be evil.

Hebrews 4:13

13 Neither is there any creature that is not manifest in his sight: but all things are naked and opened unto the eyes of him with whom we have to do.

Psalm 44:21

21 Shall not God search this out? for he knoweth the secrets of the heart.

Proverbs 25:9

9 Debate thy cause with thy neighbour himself; and discover not a secret to another:

68

SIGNATURE SCENT

You need a signature candle for your home and a signature scent for your body. Your body should always have this clean sensual smell. You should have a casual, nighttime, daytime, bedtime scent. It does not matter if you have someone significant in your life or not. Always have a clean house and a clean body. The significant other will come. Take care of your body and home. Cleanliness means being clean and free from germs and dirt from your body, mind and home.

Isaiah 1:16

[16] Wash you, make you clean; put away the evil of your doings from before mine eyes; cease to do evil;

Psalm 51:10

[10] Create in me a clean heart, O God; and renew a right spirit within me.

Psalm 51:7

7 Purge me with hyssop, and I shall be clean: wash me, and I shall be whiter than snow.

1 John 1:9

9 If we confess our sins, he is faithful and just to forgive us our sins, and to cleanse us from all unrighteousness.

2 Corinthians 7:1

1 Having therefore these promises, dearly beloved, let us cleanse ourselves from all filthiness of the flesh and spirit, perfecting holiness in the fear of God.

Deuteronomy 23:12-14

12 Thou shalt have a place also without the camp, whither thou shalt go forth abroad: 13 And thou shalt have a paddle upon thy weapon; and it shall be, when thou wilt ease thyself abroad, thou shalt dig therewith, and shalt turn back and cover that which cometh from thee: 14 For the LORD thy God walketh in the midst of thy camp, to deliver thee, and to give up thine enemies before thee; therefore shall thy camp be holy: that he see no unclean thing in thee, and turn away from thee.

<u>**Matthew 23:26**</u>

[26] Thou blind Pharisee, cleanse first that which is within the cup and platter, that the outside of them may be clean also.

69

FORCED START

Vigorously encourage others to follow their dreams. For example, your children, a late-bloomer friend, or even yourself. Some people have a failure-to-launch syndrome. They have spent a lifetime blaming their childhood and everything in between for their woes. Don't engage in their woes. Give them the push they need to move forward, or let them go. Provide help where you can, emotionally, financially and physically. However, you _must_ put a limit on this help. If you don't, you will be enabling them, instead of forcing them to follow their dreams.

Revelation 21:4

⁴ And God shall wipe away all tears from their eyes; and there shall be no more death, neither sorrow, nor crying, neither shall there be any more pain: for the former things are passed away.

Isaiah 43:18-19

¹⁸ Remember ye not the former things, neither consider the things of old. ¹⁹ Behold, I will do a

new thing; now it shall spring forth; shall ye not
know it? I will even make a way in the wilderness,
and rivers in the desert.

70

TRANSFERRED THOUGHT

When someone bullies you into following their idea, don't get bamboozled. Never let someone bully you into doing things their way. You have your own mind for a reason. Use it and follow your instinct, not someone else's. Transferred thought means you are following someone esles dream, trying to live in another person's shallow. They convinced you to go to law school, become a nurse. Your dream was to be a dancer. You are now stuck living an existence that you can't bare. Reject transferred thoughts, they will leave you misearable.

James 4:11-12

[11] Speak not evil one of another, brethren. He that speaketh evil of his brother, and judgeth his brother, speaketh evil of the law, and judgeth the law: but if thou judge the law, thou art not a doer of the law, but a judge. [12] There is one lawgiver, who is able to save and to destroy: who art thou that judgest another?

James 1:26

²⁶ If any man among you seem to be religious, and bridleth not his tongue, but deceiveth his own heart, this man's religion is vain.

Titus 3:1-3

¹ Put them in mind to be subject to principalities and powers, to obey magistrates, to be ready to every good work, ² To speak evil of no man, to be no brawlers, but gentle, shewing all meekness unto all men. ³ For we ourselves also were sometimes foolish, disobedient, deceived, serving divers lusts and pleasures, living in malice and envy, hateful, and hating one another.

Ephesians 4:31

³¹ Let all bitterness, and wrath, and anger, and clamour, and evil speaking, be put away from you, with all malice:

Ephesians 4:29

²⁹ Let no corrupt communication proceed out of your mouth, but that which is good to the use of edifying, that it may minister grace unto the hearers.

<u>**Colossians 3:8**</u>

[8] But now ye also put off all these; anger, wrath, malice, blasphemy, filthy communication out of your mouth.

71

TOGETHER, BUT SEPARATE

Living with someone as a couple but feeling totally alone. I have been there and done that, and over-stayed my welcome. A lonely relationship helps no one. Let the person go and endure the pain of the broken relationship now rather than later. Examples:

- You'll are ignoring each other
- Not speaking to each other
- Have no respect for each other
- Not fulfilling each others mental, physical and emotional needs

Hebrews 13:5-6

[5] Let your conversation be without covetousness; and be content with such things as ye have: for he hath said, I will never leave thee, nor forsake thee. [6] So that we may boldly say, The Lord is my helper, and I will not fear what man shall do unto me.

Isaiah 41:10

[10] Fear thou not; for I am with thee: be not dismayed; for I am thy God: I will strengthen thee; yea, I will help thee; yea, I will uphold thee with the right hand of my righteousness.

1 Peter 5:7

[7] Casting all your care upon him; for he careth for you.

Deuteronomy 31:6

[6] Be strong and of a good courage, fear not, nor be afraid of them: for the LORD thy God, he it is that doth go with thee; he will not fail thee, nor forsake thee.

Genesis 2:18

[18] And the LORD God said, It is not good that the man should be alone; I will make him an help meet for him.

Joshua 1:5

[5] There shall not any man be able to stand before thee all the days of thy life: as I was with Moses, so I will be with thee: I will not fail thee, nor forsake thee.

72

SIDE CHICK

This girl will accept being in second place. Some side chicks become the main chick, but there will always be a price to pay. If your man is currently in a relationship with someone else, tell him to be man enough to end that previous situation before getting it on with you. This will allow you to start with a foundation that is clean and free of any guilt. You are worth more than being a side chick. Know your worth, and stand your ground.

Matthew 19:3-9

3 The Pharisees also came unto him, tempting him, and saying unto him, Is it lawful for a man to put away his wife for every cause? 4 And he answered and said unto them, Have ye not read, that he which made them at the beginning made them male and female, 5 And said, For this cause shall a man leave father and mother, and shall cleave to his wife: and they twain shall be one flesh? 6 Wherefore they are no more twain, but one flesh. What therefore God hath joined together, let not man put asunder. 7 They say

unto him, Why did Moses then command to give a writing of divorcement, and to put her away? ⁸ He saith unto them, Moses because of the hardness of your hearts suffered you to put away your wives: but from the beginning it was not so. ⁹ And I say unto you, Whosoever shall put away his wife, except it be for fornication, and shall marry another, committeth adultery: and whoso marrieth her which is put away doth commit adultery.

73

UNRESOLVED GUILT

This is when you have wronged someone, or done something wrong. Don't allow yourself to be riddled with guilt. It is not healthy. You owe it to yourself to forgive yourself, so ask for forgiveness and move on. Unresolved guilt will destroy your future.

1 John 1:9

9 That was the true Light, which lighteth every man that cometh into the world.

Romans 8:1

1 There is therefore now no condemnation to them which are in Christ Jesus, who walk not after the flesh, but after the Spirit.

Romans 5:1

1 Therefore being justified by faith, we have peace with God through our Lord Jesus Christ:

Romans 3:23

23 For all have sinned, and come short of the glory of God;

James 4:7

7 Submit yourselves therefore to God. Resist the devil, and he will flee from you.

Luke 15:7

7 I say unto you, that likewise joy shall be in heaven over one sinner that repenteth, more than over ninety and nine just persons, which need no repentance.

James 1:14

14 But every man is tempted, when he is drawn away of his own lust, and enticed.

Psalm 103:11-12

11 For as the heaven is high above the earth, so great is his mercy toward them that fear him. 12 As far as the east is from the west, so far hath he removed our transgressions from us.

74

PROACTIVE ACTIONS

Plan ahead or plan to fail. This is a repeated theme in this book. Proactive actions, save money for the future. Take care of your body so you can live long in good health. Be kind to people and kindness will come back to you.

Proverbs 6:6-8

⁶ Go to the ant, thou sluggard; consider her ways, and be wise: ⁷ Which having no guide, overseer, or ruler, ⁸ Provideth her meat in the summer, and gathereth her food in the harvest.

Proverbs 16:3

³ Commit thy works unto the LORD, and thy thoughts shall be established.

Proverbs 16:9

⁹ A man's heart deviseth his way: but the LORD directeth his steps.

Proverbs 19:21

21 There are many devices in a man's heart; nevertheless the counsel of the LORD, that shall stand.

Proverbs 21:5

5 The thoughts of the diligent tend only to plenteousness; but of every one that is hasty only to want.

Luke 14:28

28 For which of you, intending to build a tower, sitteth not down first, and counteth the cost, whether he have sufficient to finish it?

Jeremiah 29:11

11 For I know the thoughts that I think toward you, saith the LORD, thoughts of peace, and not of evil, to give you an expected end.

James 4:13-15

13 Go to now, ye that say, To day or to morrow we will go into such a city, and continue there a year, and buy and sell, and get gain: 14 Whereas ye know not what shall be on the morrow. For what is your life? It is even a vapour, that appeareth for a little time, and then vanisheth away. 15 For that ye ought to say, If the Lord will, we shall live, and do this, or that.

75

TOTAL FORGIVENESS

Once you accept someone's apology, don't revisit the problem or situation again. Truly forgive them and let it go. Always remember forgiveness is for yourself. Not the other person. Practice forgiveness, every day and all the time.

<u>1 John 1:9-10</u>

[9] If we confess our sins, he is faithful and just to forgive us our sins, and to cleanse us from all unrighteousness. [10] If we say that we have not sinned, we make him a liar, and his word is not in us.

<u>Matthew 6:14-16</u>

[14] For if ye forgive men their trespasses, your heavenly Father will also forgive you: [15] But if ye forgive not men their trespasses, neither will your Father forgive your trespasses. [16] Moreover when ye fast, be not, as the hypocrites, of a sad

countenance: for they disfigure their faces, that they may appear unto men to fast. Verily I say unto you, They have their reward.

76

SUPERIOR THOUGHTS

This is when no one can tell you anything. You feel you are always right and can't take direction. Sooner or later, this is going to be your downfall. Even when you own your own business, you still have to work with people. The smartest businessman will always hire and work with people that are smarter than them. Don't let your thoughts and arrogance be the death of you. Everyone you meet has knowledge and experience that you can learn from.

Philippians 2:3-4

[3] Let nothing be done through strife or vainglory; but in lowliness of mind let each esteem other better than themselves. [4] Look not every man on his own things, but every man also on the things of others.

77

IGNORED INSTINCTS

God, the higher power, has equipped you with everything you need to survive in life. We all seem to learn to distrust ourselves and our inner instinct. Believe in yourself first. When the voice within is telling you to calm down, don't proceed; the voice within is trying to help you. Never ignore it. Proceed with caution and remain calm above all things. Follow God and stay humble; he will lead you in the right direction.

Genesis 1:1-3

1 In the beginning God created the heaven and the earth. 2 And the earth was without form, and void; and darkness was upon the face of the deep. And the Spirit of God moved upon the face of the waters. 3 And God said, Let there be light: and there was light.

Genesis 3:15

15 And I will put enmity between thee and the woman, and between thy seed and her seed; it

shall bruise thy head, and thou shalt bruise his heel.

Genesis 1:27

27 So God created man in his own image, in the image of God created he him; male and female created he them.

2 Timothy 3:16

16 All scripture is given by inspiration of God, and is profitable for doctrine, for reproof, for correction, for instruction in righteousness::

John 1:14

14 And the Word was made flesh, and dwelt among us, (and we beheld his glory, the glory as of the only begotten of the Father,) full of grace and truth.

78

UNDISCOVERED TALENT

Sometimes we walk around trying for a lifetime to figure out what it is we should be doing with our life. Quiet your mind and speak to the God that loves you. Understand that you can be, do and have anything you want in life. Just take a moment and be clear about what you want. You've got this, and the only one you should be in competition with at all times is yourself. Your talent will surface when you follow your heart and don't chase dollars. The money will come when you figure out what truly brings you joy, and just do it.

1 Corinthians 12:27-31

27 But God hath chosen the foolish things of the world to confound the wise; and God hath chosen the weak things of the world to confound the things which are mighty; 28 And base things of the world, and things which are despised, hath God chosen, yea, and things which are not, to bring to nought things that are: 29 That no flesh should glory in his presence. 30 But of him are ye in Christ Jesus, who of God is made unto us

wisdom, and righteousness, and sanctification, and redemption: [31] That, according as it is written, He that glorieth, let him glory in the Lord.

79

LONGTIME HOLD

You have supported everyone else your entire life. You cheered their success, weddings, marriage, job promotions, awards and all their achievements. You get my point. It's time for you to declare your turn. God sees you and has your back. Stop the madness and go for what is yours. It is your year, time, moment for the world to celebrate with you. You've held onto your dreams long enough. It's time for you to go for it.

Proverbs 3:1-6

[1] My son, forget not my law; but let thine heart keep my commandments: [2] For length of days, and long life, and peace, shall they add to thee. [3] Let not mercy and truth forsake thee: bind them about thy neck; write them upon the table of thine heart: [4] So shalt thou find favour and good understanding in the sight of God and man. [5] Trust in the LORD with all thine heart; and lean not unto thine own understanding. [6] In all thy ways acknowledge him, and he shall direct thy paths.

<u>**Hebrews 11:1**</u>

¹ Now faith is the substance of things hoped for, the evidence of things not seen.

80

SHAKEN CONFIDENCE

This is when someone close to you has let you down. They may have called you names or made you question yourself. Now you are not sure if you like yourself. Shake is off. You have got your life to live. You are good enough now; not when you get into shape; not when you grow some hair; not when you learn how to talk better. You are good enough right now, in this moment. Live in the now because you deserve it, and so do all the friends and family members that you interact with daily. You are good enough "as is". There is a saying that "hurt people, hurt people." Pray for the person that tried to steal your joy and confidence. Someone has probably tried to do the same thing to them.

Although it is never right to treat people wrong, they probably did not know any better. Take the necessary steps to build your confidence back up. You deserve to live a wonderful life. You have to create your future. Confidence is mostly described as a state of being sure about yourself, including your choices, decisions and state of being. Self-confidence is just having confidence in yourself. The opposite of confidence is being arrogant and that is not what we are trying to achieve.

<u>**Philippians 3:3**</u>

³ For we are the circumcision, which worship God in the spirit, and rejoice in Christ Jesus, and have no confidence in the flesh.

81

BROKEN SILENCE

This is when you try to be super-nice to people, and they walk all over you like a door mat. You've been quiet long enough. Pull yourself together. They have been poking at the lion's den and you allowed the lion to stay asleep. If someone has pushed the button excessively – wake up. You now have permission to unlock the door and unleash the beast. Don't be a door mat.

Proverbs 17:28

28 Even a fool, when he holdeth his peace, is counted wise: and he that shutteth his lips is esteemed a man of understanding

Lamentations 3:26

26 It is good that a man should both hope and quietly wait for the salvation of the LORD.

Psalm 46:10

¹⁰ Be still, and know that I am God: I will be exalted among the heathen, I will be exalted in the earth.

Psalm 62:5

⁵ My soul, wait thou only upon God; for my expectation is from him.

Psalm 141:3

³ Set a watch, O LORD, before my mouth; keep the door of my lips.

1 Timothy 2:11-14

¹¹ Let the woman learn in silence with all subjection. ¹² But I suffer not a woman to teach, nor to usurp authority over the man, but to be in silence. ¹³ For Adam was first formed, then Eve. ¹⁴ And Adam was not deceived, but the woman being deceived was in the transgression.

1 Corinthians 14:34-35

³⁴ Let your women keep silence in the churches: for it is not permitted unto them to speak; but they are commanded to be under obedience as also saith the law. ³⁵ And if they will learn any thing, let them ask their husbands at home: for it is a shame for women to speak in the church.

82

OPEN CRY

Sometimes you want to remain strong when you are going through challenges in life. However, God provided you with friends for a reason. Open up to a friend and just release the tears. Tears help cleanse the soul and sometimes a good cry makes us stronger. Cry and get your power back. Crying is the best thing that you can do to heal your soul. It reduces the stored-up tension, removes toxins and increases the body's ability to heal itself, physically and emotionally.

Psalm 56:8-9

[8] Thou tellest my wanderings: put thou my tears into thy bottle: are they not in thy book? [9] When I cry unto thee, then shall mine enemies turn back: this I know; for God is for me.

Revelation 21:4-5

[4] And God shall wipe away all tears from their eyes; and there shall be no more death, neither sorrow, nor crying, neither shall there be any more pain: for the former things are passed away.

[5] And he that sat upon the throne said, Behold, I make all things new. And he said unto me, Write: for these words are true and faithful.

John 11:34-35

[34] And said, Where have ye laid him? They said unto him, Lord, come and see. [35] Jesus wept.

83

CALMED VICTORY

This is when you let God fight your battles. No matter what storm you go through, at the end the victory will be yours. Don't boast about your victory, rejoice in calmness. Praise God and give him all the glory. You can't do better than God when it comes to fighting your enemies. Let God fight your battle; he doesn't need your help.

Deuteronomy 20:1-4

1 When thou goest out to battle against thine enemies, and seest horses, and chariots, and a people more than thou, be not afraid of them: for the LORD thy God is with thee, which brought thee up out of the land of Egypt. 2 And it shall be, when ye are come nigh unto the battle, that the priest shall approach and speak unto the people, 3 And shall say unto them, Hear, O Israel, ye approach this day unto battle against your enemies: let not your hearts faint, fear not, and do not tremble, neither be ye terrified because of them; 4 For the LORD your God is he that goeth with you, to fight for you against your enemies, to save you.

84

WATER JUNKIE

Protect your temple with everything in you. Become a water junkie and try your best to drink one gallon of water per day. I try my best. Sometimes I fall short but fight every day to meet the goal. Use a fresh lemon in the water or cucumber - whatever it takes. Just drink your water all day long, responsibly.

1 Corinthians 6:12-20

12 All things are lawful unto me, but all things are not expedient: all things are lawful for me, but I will not be brought under the power of any. 13 Meats for the belly, and the belly for meats: but God shall destroy both it and them. Now the body is not for fornication, but for the Lord; and the Lord for the body. 14 And God hath both raised up the Lord, and will also raise up us by his own power. 15 Know ye not that your bodies are the members of Christ? shall I then take the members of Christ, and make them the members of an harlot? God forbid. 16 What? know ye not that he which is joined to an harlot is one body?

for two, saith he, shall be one flesh. [17] But he that is joined unto the Lord is one spirit. [18] Flee fornication. Every sin that a man doeth is without the body; but he that committeth fornication sinneth against his own body. [19] What? know ye not that your body is the temple of the Holy Ghost which is in you, which ye have of God, and ye are not your own? [20] For ye are bought with a price: therefore glorify God in your body, and in your spirit, which are God's.

85

SCARFACE THEORY

Everybody loves gangster movies, and some try to be like a gangster in life. Before you do this, fast forward to the end of the story. Scarface dies in the end. Pull yourself together and just be yourself. You are good enough. You don't have to pretend to be someone that you are not.

Matthew 5:38-39

[38] Ye have heard that it hath been said, An eye for an eye, and a tooth for a tooth: [39] But I say unto you, That ye resist not evil: but whosoever shall smite thee on thy right cheek, turn to him the other also.

Exodus 21:24

[24] Eye for eye, tooth for tooth, hand for hand, foot for foot,

Romans 12:10-21

[10] Be kindly affectioned one to another with brotherly love; in honour preferring one another; [11] Not slothful in business; fervent in spirit; serving the Lord; [12] Rejoicing in hope; patient in tribulation; continuing instant in prayer; [13] Distributing to the necessity of saints; given to hospitality. [14] Bless them which persecute you: bless, and curse not. [15] Rejoice with them that do rejoice, and weep with them that weep. [16] Be of the same mind one toward another. Mind not high things, but condescend to men of low estate. Be not wise in your own conceits. [17] Recompense to no man evil for evil. Provide things honest in the sight of all men. [18] If it be possible, as much as lieth in you, live peaceably with all men. [19] Dearly beloved, avenge not yourselves, but rather give place unto wrath: for it is written, Vengeance is mine; I will repay, saith the Lord. [20] Therefore if thine enemy hunger, feed him; if he thirst, give him drink: for in so doing thou shalt heap coals of fire on his head. [21] Be not overcome of evil, but overcome evil with good.

1 Thessalonians 5:15

[15] See that none render evil for evil unto any man; but ever follow that which is good, both among yourselves, and to all men.

Proverbs 13:3

³ He that keepeth his mouth keepeth his life: but he that openeth wide his lips shall have destruction.

86

TEMPORARILY UNORGANIZED

This is the time when you seem unable to get back on track. You're forgetting important things. You're not giving 100% in any part of your life. Step back, adjust and make the necessary changes to get yourself back on track. This is your life. Participate in it.

1 Corinthians 14:33

33 For God is not the author of confusion, but of peace, as in all churches of the saints.

1 Corinthians 14:40

40 Let all things be done decently and in order.

Luke 14:28-30

28 For which of you, intending to build a tower, sitteth not down first, and counteth the cost, whether he have sufficient to finish it? 29 Lest haply, after he hath laid the foundation, and is not able to finish it, all that behold it begin to

mock him, ³⁰ Saying, This man began to build, and was not able to finish.

Habakkuk 2:2

² And the Lord answered me, and said, Write the vision, and make it plain upon tables, that he may run that readeth it.

Acts 20:28

²⁸ Take heed therefore unto yourselves, and to all the flock, over the which the Holy Ghost hath made you overseers, to feed the church of God, which he hath purchased with his own blood.

Proverbs 31:10-13

¹⁰ Who can find a virtuous woman? for her price is far above rubies. ¹¹ The heart of her husband doth safely trust in her, so that he shall have no need of spoil. ¹² She will do him good and not evil all the days of her life. ¹³ She seeketh wool, and flax, and worketh willingly with her hands.

87

AMATEUR VIBES

This is when you allow yourself to get sucked in by people that don't deserve your energy or time. They are draining you. Acknowledge, their presence, and tell them to move on – and then ignore them. You don't have time for energy suckers. Drop them like a bad habit.

1 Corinthians 15:33

33 Be not deceived: evil communications corrupt good manners.

Proverbs 22:24

24 Make no friendship with an angry man; and with a furious man thou shalt not go:

Matthew 7:1-2

1 Judge not, that ye be not judged. 2 For with what judgment ye judge, ye shall be judged: and with what measure ye mete, it shall be measured to you again.

Matthew 11:28

28 Come unto me, all ye that labour and are heavy laden, and I will give you rest.

Mark 7:20-23

20 And he said, That which cometh out of the man, that defileth the man. 21 For from within, out of the heart of men, proceed evil thoughts, adulteries, fornications, murders, 22 Thefts, covetousness, wickedness, deceit, lasciviousness, an evil eye, blasphemy, pride, foolishness: 23 All these evil things come from within, and defile the man.

Galatians 5:19-21

19 Now the works of the flesh are manifest, which are these; Adultery, fornication, uncleanness, lasciviousness, 20 Idolatry, witchcraft, hatred, variance, emulations, wrath, strife, seditions, heresies, 21 Envying's, murders, drunkenness, reveling, and such like: of the which I tell you before, as I have also told you in time past, that they which do such things shall not inherit the kingdom of God.

Deuteronomy 7:26

26 Neither shalt thou bring an abomination into thine house, lest thou be a cursed thing like it: but thou shalt utterly detest it, and thou shalt utterly abhor it; for it is a cursed thing.

88

UNKNOWLEDGEABLE

This is when you have to ignore people for your own good. You must not acknowledge them after you have told them. They are now dead to you. Don't ever acknowledge them again. This is for those people that pretend to be in your corner, but talk about you behind your back. Don't acknowledge them, they aren't worth your time.

2 Timothy 2:15

15 Study to shew thyself approved unto God, a workman that needeth not to be ashamed, rightly dividing the word of truth.

2 Timothy 3:16

16 All scripture is given by inspiration of God, and is profitable for doctrine, for reproof, for correction, for instruction in righteousness:

Deuteronomy 12:32

[32] What thing soever I command you, observe to do it: thou shalt not add thereto, nor diminish from it.

Exodus 20:1-4

1 And God spake all these words, saying, [2] I am the LORD thy God, which have brought thee out of the land of Egypt, out of the house of bondage. [3] Thou shalt have no other gods before me. [4] Thou shalt not make unto thee any graven image, or any likeness of any thing that is in heaven above, or that is in the earth beneath, or that is in the water under the earth.

Colossians 3:17

[17] And whatsoever ye do in word or deed, do all in the name of the Lord Jesus, giving thanks to God and the Father by him.

89

OUT OF SORTS

Not physically looking like yourself. Invest in your body and do whatever it takes to get things right. Exercise, eat right and treat yourself kindly. Look in the mirror every day and tell yourself how great you are.

1 Samuel 16:7

7 But the LORD said unto Samuel, Look not on his countenance, or on the height of his stature; because I have refused him: for the LORD seeth not as man seeth; for man looketh on the outward appearance, but the LORD looketh on the heart.

1 Peter 3:3-4

3 Whose adorning let it not be that outward adorning of plaiting the hair, and of wearing of gold, or of putting on of apparel; 4 But let it be the hidden man of the heart, in that which is not corruptible, even the ornament of a meek and quiet spirit, which is in the sight of God of great price.

Psalm 139:14

[14] I will praise thee; for I am fearfully and wonderfully made: marvellous are thy works; and that my soul knoweth right well.

1 Corinthians 6:19-20

[19] What? know ye not that your body is the temple of the Holy Ghost which is in you, which ye have of God, and ye are not your own? [20] For ye are bought with a price: therefore glorify God in your body, and in your spirit, which are God's.

Proverbs 31:30

[30] Favour is deceitful, and beauty is vain: but a woman that feareth the Lord, she shall be praised.

1 Timothy 4:8

[8] For bodily exercise profiteth little: but godliness is profitable unto all things, having promise of the life that now is, and of that which is to come.

90

RETHINK YOUR RESOURCES

Sometimes you have to dump some friends. Cut people off like Verizon would, if you did not pay your bill. Sometimes the resources may not be other people it may be yourself. You can train your mind to think positive and do better.

Proverbs 3:1-5

¹ My son, forget not my law; but let thine heart keep my commandments: ² For length of days, and long life, and peace, shall they add to thee. ³ Let not mercy and truth forsake thee: bind them about thy neck; write them upon the table of thine heart: ⁴ So shalt thou find favour and good understanding in the sight of God and man. ⁵ Trust in the Lord with all thine heart; and lean not unto thine own understanding.

John 10:35

³⁵ If he called them gods, unto whom the word of God came, and the scripture cannot be broken;

<u>**Matthew 28:19-20**</u>

[19]Go ye therefore, and teach all nations, baptizing them in the name of the Father, and of the Son, and of the Holy Ghost: [20] Teaching them to observe all things whatsoever I have commanded you: and, lo, I am with you always, even unto the end of the world. Amen.

91

SELECTIVE PURGING

Eradicate the bad things in you and support and nurture the good things. Let good rise above evil all the time.

2 Timothy 2:21

²¹ If a man therefore purge himself from these, he shall be a vessel unto honour, sanctified, and meet for the master's use, and prepared unto every good work.

John 15:2

² Every branch in me that beareth not fruit he taketh away: and every branch that beareth fruit, he purgeth it, that it may bring forth more fruit.

Ezekiel 20:38

³⁸ And I will purge out from among you the rebels, and them that transgress against me: I will bring them forth out of the country where they

sojourn, and they shall not enter into the land of Israel: and ye shall know that I am the Lord.

1 John 1:7

7 But if we walk in the light, as he is in the light, we have fellowship one with another, and the blood of Jesus Christ his Son cleanseth us from all sin.

Hebrews 9:22

22 And almost all things are by the law purged with blood; and without shedding of blood is no remission.

92

ECONOMICALLY STABLE

Your situation when someone asks about your finances. This is how you want to be, whether or not you are in a relationship. You want to be able to take care of yourself at all times. There was a time when I was in a relationship and my lifestyle was highly dependent upon my significant other. I felt secure knowing that he was my back up. When the relationship ended, I was emotionally, physically and financially unstable. It was the worst feeling in the world. Don't ever put yourself in this situation. Save your money and be prepared for anything that might come your way.

Hebrews 13:5

5 Let your conversation be without covetousness; and be content with such things as ye have: for he hath said, I will never leave thee, nor forsake thee.

1 Timothy 6:10

10 For the love of money is the root of all evil: which while some coveted after, they have erred

from the faith, and pierced themselves through with many sorrows.

Proverbs 13:11

[11] Wealth gotten by vanity shall be diminished: but he that gathereth by labour shall increase.

Proverbs 22:7

[7] The rich ruleth over the poor, and the borrower is servant to the lender.

Ecclesiastes 5:10

[10] He that loveth silver shall not be satisfied with silver; nor he that loveth abundance with increase: this is also vanity.

Matthew 6:19-21

[19] Lay not up for yourselves treasures upon earth, where moth and rust doth corrupt, and where thieves break through and steal: [20] But lay up for yourselves treasures in heaven, where neither moth nor rust doth corrupt, and where thieves do not break through nor steal: [21] For where your treasure is, there will your heart be also.

93

CLOSED CHAPTER

Sometimes, you have to let go of a long-term or short-term relationship. Close the chapter, burn the book, and move on. One of my favorite pictures that is roaming the internet is this picture of Jesus holding a huge teddy bear behind his back. He is trying to convince a little girl to give him the small teddy bear she is holding in her hand. She keeps telling God, "But I love it." If only she knew what God had behind His back for her, she would gladly give up the teddy bear! Always trust God, and know that He has something better in store for you. Close the chapter on the old and have mustard seed faith that something greater awaits you.

Romans 8:18

18 For I reckon that the sufferings of this present time are not worthy to be compared with the glory which shall be revealed in us.

Romans 12:9

9 Let love be without dissimulation. Abhor that which is evil; cleave to that which is good.

Philippians 3:14

¹⁴ I press toward the mark for the prize of the high calling of God in Christ Jesus.

Philippians 4:6

⁶ Be careful for nothing; but in every thing by prayer and supplication with thanksgiving let your requests be made known unto God.

Jeremiah 29:11

¹¹ For I know the thoughts that I think toward you, saith the LORD, thoughts of peace, and not of evil, to give you an expected end.

Isaiah 43:18-20

¹⁸ Remember ye not the former things, neither consider the things of old. ¹⁹ Behold, I will do a new thing; now it shall spring forth; shall ye not know it? I will even make a way in the wilderness, and rivers in the desert. ²⁰ The beast of the field shall honour me, the dragons and the owls: because I give waters in the wilderness, and rivers in the desert, to give drink to my people, my chosen.

94

ENCOURAGED ADVENTURE

This is when your friends, family and loved ones support you stepping out of your comfort zone. Trust the process. You can do it! Lean on your family, if necessary, but write the book, take the acting class, start your journey to health. Just do it and never give up.

Ecclesiastes 2:22-25

22 For what hath man of all his labour, and of the vexation of his heart, wherein he hath laboured under the sun? 23 For all his days are sorrows, and his travail grief; yea, his heart taketh not rest in the night. This is also vanity. 24 There is nothing better for a man, than that he should eat and drink, and that he should make his soul enjoy good in his labour. This also I saw, that it was from the hand of God. 25 For who can eat, or who else can hasten hereunto, more than I?

Ecclesiastes 3:12-13

¹² I know that there is no good in them, but for a man to rejoice, and to do good in his life. ¹³ And also that every man should eat and drink, and enjoy the good of all his labour, it is the gift of God.

Ecclesiastes 5:18-20

¹⁸ Behold that which I have seen: it is good and comely for one to eat and to drink, and to enjoy the good of all his labour that he taketh under the sun all the days of his life, which God giveth him: for it is his portion. ¹⁹ Every man also to whom God hath given riches and wealth, and hath given him power to eat thereof, and to take his portion, and to rejoice in his labour; this is the gift of God. ²⁰ For he shall not much remember the days of his life; because God answereth him in the joy of his heart.

Ecclesiastes 8:15

¹⁵ Then I commended mirth, because a man hath no better thing under the sun, than to eat, and to drink, and to be merry: for that shall abide with him of his labour the days of his life, which God giveth him under the sun.

95

SNAIL PACE

Slow and steady really does win the race. Don't get frustrated with the process. If weight loss is your battle, you might be losing just one pound a week. That's okay. You now weigh one pound less than the week before. Remember, no matter what situation you are currently in, you did not get there overnight. You took the local train to that situation, and now you're going to have to take the local train to get out of it.

James 1:19

¹⁹ Wherefore, my beloved brethren, let every man be swift to hear, slow to speak, slow to wrath:

Jeremiah 2:2

² Go and cry in the ears of Jerusalem, saying, Thus saith the Lord; I remember thee, the kindness of thy youth, the love of thine espousals, when thou wentest after me in the wilderness, in a land that was not sown.

96

OVERDOSE ON SELF-HELP

There are tons of great self-help books out there that can help to get you back on track. So many have helped me in my journey. Self-help books can provide hope, help change your mindset, and give you all the help you need to get back on track.

John 14:13-14

[13] And whatsoever ye shall ask in my name, that will I do, that the Father may be glorified in the Son. [14] If ye shall ask any thing in my name, I will do it.

Psalm 121:1-8

1 I will lift up mine eyes unto the hills, from whence cometh my help. [2] My help cometh from the LORD, which made heaven and earth. [3] He will not suffer thy foot to be moved: he that keepeth thee will not slumber. [4] Behold, he that keepeth Israel shall neither slumber nor sleep. [5] The LORD is thy keeper: the LORD is thy shade upon thy right hand. **⁶** The sun shall not smite thee by day, nor the moon by night. **⁷** The LORD shall preserve thee from all evil: he shall preserve thy soul. **⁸** The LORD shall preserve thy going out and thy coming in from this time forth, and even for evermore.

Matthew 11:28

²⁸ Come unto me, all ye that labour and are heavy laden, and I will give you rest.

Matthew 7:7

⁷ Ask, and it shall be given you; seek, and ye shall find; knock, and it shall be opened unto you:

Jeremiah 31:16

¹⁶ Thus saith the LORD; Refrain thy voice from weeping, and thine eyes from tears: for thy work shall be rewarded, saith the LORD; and they shall come again from the land of the enemy.

97

CHOSEN PASSION

God wants you to be happy. His only plan is for you to win. Go deep within your soul. Find your passion. Work every day to cultivate it. Write it down and create your winning vision board. I am praying that you win – go with your passion.

1 Corinthians 6:12

^{12} All things are lawful unto me, but all things are not expedient: all things are lawful for me, but I will not be brought under the power of any.

John 14:6

^{6} Jesus saith unto him, I am the way, the truth, and the life: no man cometh unto the Father, but by me.

John 10:1-2

^{1} Verily, verily, I say unto you, He that entereth not by the door into the sheepfold, but climbeth up some other way, the same is a thief and a robber. ² But he that entereth in by the door is the shepherd of the sheep.

John 6:53

⁵³ Then Jesus said unto them, Verily, verily, I say unto you, Except ye eat the flesh of the Son of man, and drink his blood, ye have no life in you.

Luke 10:25

²⁵ And, behold, a certain lawyer stood up, and tempted him, saying, Master, what shall I do to inherit eternal life?

98

LAUGH EVERY DAY

Find something to laugh about every day. Laugher heals the soul. Watch funny movies. Attend comedy shows. Just have fun and laugh, laugh, laugh and laugh some more.

Proverbs 17:22

[22] A merry heart doeth good like a medicine: but a broken spirit drieth the bones.

99

DEDICATED LOYALTY

Be a loyal friend. Loyal wife, loyal husband, loyal mate or loyal whatever you are. Loyalty is everything.

Proverbs 17:17

[17] A friend loveth at all times, and a brother is born for adversity.

Proverbs 18:24

[24] A man that hath friends must shew himself friendly: and there is a friend that sticketh closer than a brother.

Proverbs 21:21

[21] He that followeth after righteousness and mercy findeth life, righteousness, and honour.

Ruth 1:16-17

[16] And Ruth said, Intreat me not to leave thee, or to return from following after thee: for whither thou goest, I will go; and where thou lodgest, I will lodge: thy people shall be my people, and thy God my God: [17] Where thou diest, will I die, and there will I be buried: the LORD do so to me, and more also, if ought but death part thee and me.

1 Corinthians 16:13-14

[13] Watch ye, stand fast in the faith, quit you like men, be strong. [14] Let all your things be done with charity.

Matthew 26:35

[35] Peter said unto him, Though I should die with thee, yet will I not deny thee. Likewise also said all the disciples.

Matthew 18:15

[15] Moreover if thy brother shall trespass against thee, go and tell him his fault between thee and him alone: if he shall hear thee, thou hast gained thy brother.

Matthew 26:33

[33] Peter answered and said unto him, Though all men shall be offended because of thee, yet will I never be offended.

100

EXPLAINED FORGIVENESS

Forgive those that forgive you, and even those that don't. Forgiveness is *a gift to yourself.* It's destructive to go around holding hatred in your heart, mind, body and soul. Its damages you more than the other person. Forgive, and set yourself free.

Mark 11:25

25 And when ye stand praying, forgive, if ye have ought against any: that your Father also which is in heaven may forgive you your trespasses.

Ephesians 4:32

32 And be ye kind one to another, tenderhearted, forgiving one another, even as God for Christ's sake hath forgiven you.

1 John 1:9

⁹ If we confess our sins, he is faithful and just to forgive us our sins, and to cleanse us from all unrighteousness.

Matthew 6:14-15

¹⁴ For if ye forgive men their trespasses, your heavenly Father will also forgive you: ¹⁵ But if ye forgive not men their trespasses, neither will your Father forgive your trespasses.

Matthew 18:21-22

²⁰ For where two or three are gathered together in my name, there am I in the midst of them. ²¹ Then came Peter to him, and said, Lord, how oft shall my brother sin against me, and I forgive him? till seven times? ²² Jesus saith unto him, I say not unto thee, Until seven times: but, Until seventy times seven.

Luke 6:37

³⁷ Judge not, and ye shall not be judged: condemn not, and ye shall not be condemned: forgive, and ye shall be forgiven:

101

DOING THE WRONG THING RIGHT

This is when you know what you are doing is wrong but you do it in a right way.

- Running late for work, you decide to stop and get your favorite coffee, pick up some donuts for the team/co-workers ~ doing the wrong thing right
- Dating several people at the same time, make sure everyone is aware of the situation

102

WRITTEN WITH LOVE

This is when you write a note, letter, text, social media post with your heart and soul. Letting your authethic self shine. You are giving people a peak into your soul by letting them in when they read your written word.

103

TRICK BAG

This is when someone tries to drag you into a scheme and they know it's a scheme where you will lose your time, money and intregrity. If something does not feel right, it probably isn't right. Go with your gut, it will never lead you in the wrong direction.

104

TWO CAN BE TRUE

He/she can love two people at the same time. He/she can misrepresent the truth with you and be truthful to someone else. He/she can be a genius at work and be a terrible wife/husband.

DEAD BODIES

This is when you leave a relationship in shambles. Burn bridges in relationships and jobs. It will come back to haunt you. The skeletons and bones will come out the closet and linger in your life until you make atonement with your past. You never know who you may need to ask for a favor. A job that you may need to ask for a reference and/or work for again. **Don't leave dead bodies behind.**

Ladies and gentlemen, that is the end. I am so grateful and excited that you purchased my book. I hope you had fun reading it and I hope you use some or all of my sayings in your everyday life.

Laugh, have fun and live a long prosperous life.
With Love

Cheryl Lynn McPherson

The Grey Haired Diva

ABOUT THE AUTHOR

Cheryl McPherson is a single mother of one. Christian is her Sonshine. She is a registered nurse, loving sister, mother, daughter, cousin and friend. She loves to travel and collect art. Cheryl is a new author with aspirations of writing books that make people smile, laugh and share with friends and family.

She is positive about every aspect of life. She loves to read, write and dream about the present and future. She tries her best to live in the "NOW" with no regrets. She loves to talk and listen to her family and friends. Cheryl enjoys watching the sunrise and sunset. Spring, Summer and Fall are her favorite seasons. The winter's she can do without. Cheryl loves delicious foods and is striving to become a vegan (pray for her). Sexy shoes, romantic nights by a fireplace, a good book and fun vacations are what she lives for. Follow Cheryl on the below social media platforms.

Contact Information
Email: Cherry.mac@hotmail.com
Facebook: Author Cheryl McPherson
Instagram: The Grey Head Diva
YouTube: Chronicles of the Grey Haired Diva